The Snake Fence

A NOVEL

by
Janet Kastner Olshewsky

Printed in the United States of America
Quaker Bridge Media of Friends General Conference
1216 Arch Street, 2B
Philadelphia, PA 19107

Composition and design by David Botwinik

ISBN 978-1-937768-13-3
eISBN 978-1-937768-14-0

Library of Congress Cataloging-in-Publication Data

Kastner, Janet, 1935-
The snake fence : a novel / by Janet Kastner Olshewsky.
p. cm.

Summary: In pre-Revolutionary Pennsylvania young Noble Butler, a farm boy, encounters ideas about the rights of settlers and of Indians that challenge his Quaker values.

ISBN 978-1-937768-13-3 (pbk.)—ISBN 978-1-937768-14-0 (epub)

1. Frontier and pioneer life—Pennsylvania—Fiction. 2. Quakers—Fiction .3. Self-actualization (Psychology)—Fiction. 4. Reconciliation—Fiction. 5. Delaware Indians—Fiction. 6. Indians of North America—Pennsylvania—Fiction. 7. Pennsylvania—History—Colonial period, ca. 1600-1775—Fiction. 8. United States—History—French and Indian War, 1754-1763—Fiction.] I. Title.

PZ7.O15628Sn 2012
[Fic]—dc23

2012041873

To order more copies of this publication or other Quaker titles call 1-800-966-4556 or visit the online catalog at www.quakerbooks.org.

CONTENTS

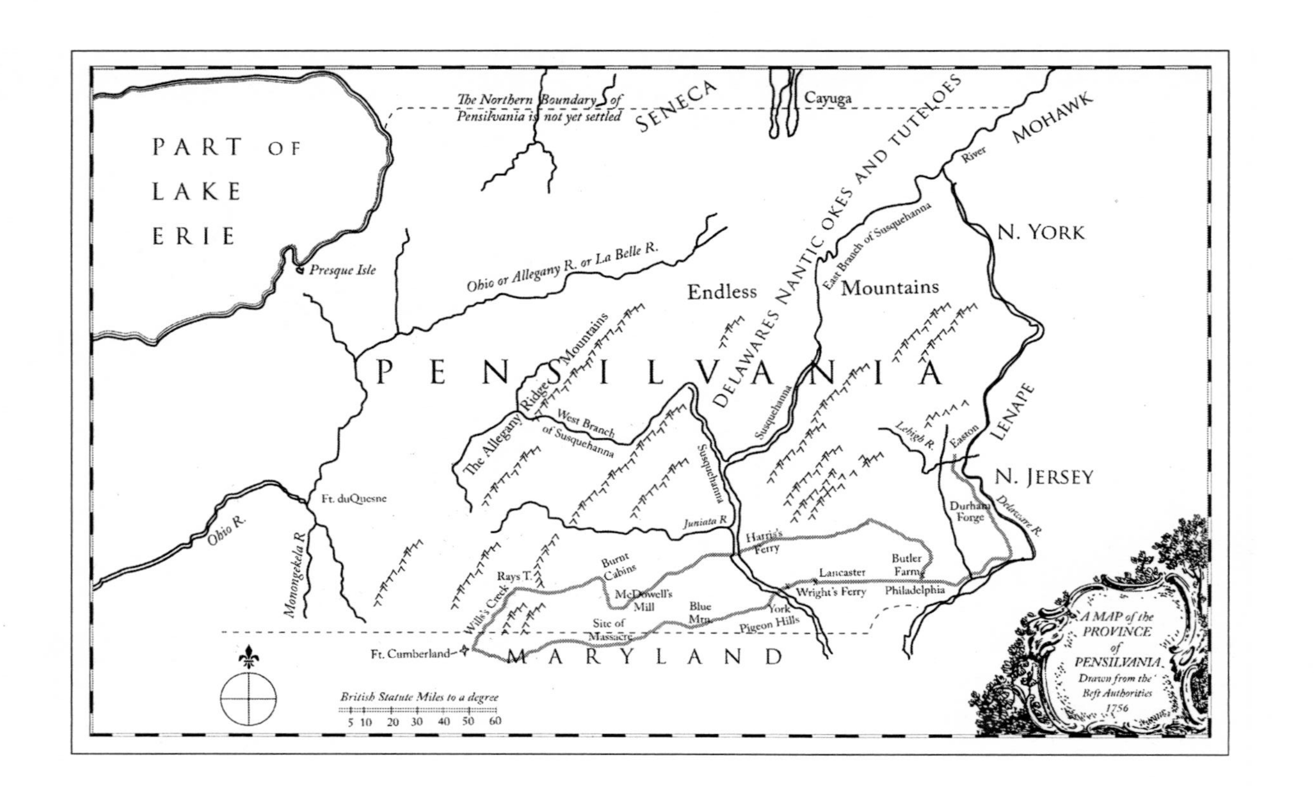
A MAP of the PROVINCE of PENSILVANIA. Drawn from the Beſt Authorities 1756
PART OF LAKE ERIE
Presque Isle
The Northern Boundary of Pensilvania is not yet settled
SENECA
Cayuga
DELAWARES NANTIC OKES AND TUTELOES
MOHAWK
River
N. YORK
Obio or Allegany R. or La Belle R.
Endless
Mountains
East Branch of Susquehanna
PENSILVANIA
The Allegany Ridge Mountains
West Branch of Susquehanna
Susquehanna
LENAPE
Lehigh R.
Easton
N. JERSEY
Durham Forge
Delaware R.
Ft. duQuesne
Obio R.
Monongekela R
Juniata R.
Harris's Ferry
Burnt Cabins
Rays T.
McDowell's Mill
Blue Mtn.
Lancaster
Butler Farm
Wright's Ferry
Philadelphia
York
Pigeon Hills
Wills's Creek
Site of Massacre
Ft. Cumberland
MARYLAND
British Statute Miles to a degree
5 10 20 30 40 50 60

PROLOGUE

"What's this, Pa?" I asked.

"Open it," he said.

I untied the string and carefully removed the brown wrapping paper. Inside was a tall narrow book bound in leather. There was no writing inside. All the pages were blank.

I looked at Pa with questions on my face.

"It's an account book, Noble," Pa said. "Thee is sixteen now, a finished apprentice, so thee should keep accounts, to know where thee stands."

"Where I stand?" I was still confused.

"Every time thee makes any financial transaction, write it in this book. When thee makes something for a customer, set down its value and how he will recompense thee. If thee owes ought to anyone, write it as thy debt. Debits on one side, credits on the facing page. Then on any given day, thee will know thy worth."

Where did I stand? What was my worth? I longed to know. Pa was thinking of money, as he always did, but I wondered where I stood on bigger questions. And whether I was worth anything at all.

At that moment, I had nothing to write in the book. My apprentice piece was a table, an unusual assignment for a mere carpenter. Mostly, carpenters do rougher work, like framing a house or building a shed. My table was beautiful, the boards invisibly joined, the legs turned on the lathe, the finish smooth to the touch. Making it had given me the dream of becoming a cabinetmaker, or joiner. But then my master sold the table, kept the money, and my apprenticeship was ended. I was a trained carpenter, but who would hire me as a journeyman without my own tools? And without a job, how could I buy tools? And how could I afford to get more training to become a cabinetmaker?

So Pa had said, "Come home and work on the farm with thy brothers and me. The way will become clear. Bide thy time."

For how long? Till I forgot all my woodworking skills and could do naught but farm? I was stuck, sitting on the snake fence between childhood and manhood. I was ready to earn a living like a man. But here I was back home again, taking orders from Pa. There was a whole world out there, and I wanted to be part of it. There were problems to solve and dangers to overcome. Could I make a difference in anything?

"Thankee, Pa," I said half-heartedly. "I'll keep accounts."

I took the new book upstairs to the bedroom I shared with Ben and put it on the low desk. Idly, I turned the blank pages and wondered how I would fill them. There were enough to last a lifetime, I thought.

Earn and spend. That's all Pa thought about.

Then a new idea struck me. I did want to know where I stood and what I was worth, but in a different way. These pages could carry more than one kind of account.

CHAPTER 1
Wagoners Wanted

Clutching both reins, I yelled, "Giddyup, Hope! Home, Seth! Faster! Faster!" Benjamin Franklin's *Pennsylvania Gazette* was tucked inside my shirt. Bags of newly milled flour thudded against the bed of Pa's old farm wagon. My teeth rattled as the horses pounded the dirt road. *Here's my chance*, I thought, *if only Pa will let me go!*

My straw hat slipped off the back of my head and my hair whipped across my eyes. I brushed it back with my forearm, not letting go of the reins.

Bad things were happening on Pennsylvania's frontier. Indians were killing people, burning houses and crops. Not here in Chester County, but in the Back Counties. And the English were sending a grand army to defend us.

Because we are Quakers and don't believe in war, I couldn't join the army. But I sure wanted to help make things right. If Indians attacked our farm, would we defend ourselves? If we didn't, what would happen? Bloody scenes flashed through my mind.

I loved my family too much to let something that awful happen without trying to . . . to what? To kill to avoid being killed? Could I even do that? If I did, the Meeting might disown me. That in itself would be a kind of death.

I had never met an Indian. At Quaker Meeting, I heard that they, like everyone else, had "that of God" within them. But the *Pennsylvania Gazette* painted a different picture. Why were Indians suddenly violent? Mayhap others had it right: they were just savages who couldn't be trusted. I was sitting on the snake fence on this issue.

People I knew seemed more interested in following Quaker teachings than in questioning them. Not everyone in the world believes as Quakers do. What makes Quakers so sure they have the Truth and everyone else is wrong? But when I asked Pa, he just looked at Ma as if to say, "Where did *this* young'un come from?" So I didn't ask again, but I kept wondering. I didn't expect to find answers at home on the farm.

Mayhap Franklin's advertisement would make all the difference. But I would have to put it to Pa in just the right way. Pa was a good man, but not easy. He had an edge in his voice, a challenging look in his eyes. He was fair but tough, and he lacked patience with anything he considered a hare-brained idea.

According to Pa, I had come up with more than my share of those ideas. One was to mount chair legs on curved runners so the chair could tilt back and forth. I still thought it was worth pursuing, but Pa had really scorned that one. "Why would I want to tilt my chair back and forth? When I sit down, I want rest, not exercise!"

I hoped this latest idea was not hare brained. It was Benjamin Franklin's idea, after all. I just wanted to be part of it. I wanted to be part of something big.

The late afternoon sun winked through little spring leaves as I careened up the hill to our barn. My fingers fumbled unhitching and watering the horses. Then I raced down to the house, jerked a dripping bucket of water from the well, splashed my sweaty face, and burst through the kitchen door. The *Pennsylvania Gazette* was hidden in my shirt.

The family had just finished supper. Everyone was there, even my oldest brother Enoch and his wife, Deborah. Pa and Ma sat in their chairs at either end of the long plank table. Bersheba and Will, older than I, and our younger brother Benjamin were perched on stools on either side. My place was still set.

"Time for the Bible reading, Noble," Pa said. "Eat thy supper while I read."

I squatted on my stool. My knees bumped up under the table now that I'd grown taller. Ma passed me a plate of bread and sausage gravy.

Pa read from the big Bible, as he did every day. Then he prayed and the family all said "Amen," same as every day. Then he put the Bible back in its heavy wooden box. Time to make my move.

"Pa," I said, "I brought home the new *Pennsylvania Gazette*. Want to read it?"

Pa put his glasses back on his nose, and Will and Ben breathed a sigh of relief. Listening to news beat going out for evening chores.

Pa opened the paper and began to read aloud. Never ones to sit idle, the women took out their needlework. My older brothers either leaned their elbows on the table or tipped their stools back against the blue hutch.

I had a plan, if I could just be patient enough. I hoped my voice wouldn't crack. It hadn't for a while now, but it still did when I least expected it.

Pa droned on about the latest squabble between the Pennsylvania Assembly and the governor. This whole year of 1755 had been full of war talk. I knew Pa would read all the news before he got to the advertisement that had captured my imagination.

Pa always read the ads. There were descriptions of runaway apprentices, indentured servants, and horses. Who knew when we might see one of them and be able to claim the reward? "Keep eyes sharp, lads," Pa would say.

He read all notices of sales of farms, houses, and estates. Not that he wanted to buy, but he wanted to know what the market was. Pa had a reputation for making money where others might not think to try or want to take the risk.

A sudden change in Pa's voice caught everyone's attention. He had found the advertisement signed by Benjamin Franklin himself.

> "Forty-one Wagons are immediately wanted, to carry a load of Oats and Indian Corn from Philadelphia to Wills's Creek, for which they are to be paid twelve pounds each wagon. Protections and passes will be given the Wagoners by authority of the General, to prevent their being impressed, or detained after delivery of their Loads. They are to set out together on Thursday the 29th instant. Apply to Benjamin Franklin, in Philadelphia. Note: several neighbors may conveniently join in fitting out a wagon, as was lately done in the Back Counties. If the Wagons cannot thus be obtained, there must be an Impress."

Pa's voice was heavy with significance as he read that last word. Leaning back in his armchair, he looked over his spectacles. The family silently considered what he had just read. I forced myself to keep quiet. I mustn't be in a hurry.

"What's an impress, Pa?" Ben asked.

"It means the army could force farmers to deliver grain, willing or not."

"And General Braddock might keep the horses and wagon, maybe even the farmer, for as long as needed," added Enoch. Even though he and Deborah were expecting a child of their own, he still enjoyed frightening Ben.

"If Indians are attacking as close as the Susquehanna, how much longer will we be safe here in Chester County?" Ma worried.

"An army must be splendid, all those uniforms, horses, and guns," Ben sighed.

"An army isn't splendid, Ben," William scoffed. "When thee sees an army, thee is seeing men who kill each other. We don't believe in war, remember."

I glared at him. "But soldiers and their horses need to eat, surely," I said. "We can't fight, but we can feed them, can't we?"

"Making money on the war," Will grumbled. "That's as bad as fighting."

"The army is already here, to defend us. Why shouldn't we feed them?" Enoch said. "Don't we owe them that?"

"But, Pa, isn't supplying an army the same as fighting?" Will asked.

I couldn't wait for Pa to answer. "Nay, Will, think of it this way: it would be unchristian to let soldiers starve in the wilderness, wouldn't it, Pa?"

Pa looked from one of us to the other, a hint of a smile on his face. He enjoyed watching us argue. It sharpened our minds, he said, though Ma pleaded with him not to encourage us. Finally he said, "The Lord wants us to be good stewards. If an opportunity comes along and does no one harm, I find naught wrong with it. "*Twelve pounds and safe passage for any who would drive a wagon loaded with oats and corn,*" Pa read again.

I had waited long enough. About to burst with excitement, I chose my words carefully, watching Pa's face for any reaction. "Pa, since thee bought the new wagon, don't we have a spare one?"

"Aye, we do."

I couldn't help wriggling on my seat. "And now that Ben is getting so stout, might thee spare me to make this trip?"

"What? That would leave me with just Will and Ben to help out here."

"Aye, but we've nearly finished planting, so there is only haying to do in Sixth Month. Sheba can help with that, and I'd be back before time to pull flax and cut rye."

"And what will draw the wagon?" Pa replied. "I can't spare two horses."

Enoch broke in. "Deborah's brother Jonathan has a horse he might let us use, if thee could spare one."

"*Us*? Does thee think to go with me?" Suddenly I saw my twelve pounds halved.

"Nay, little brother, I may let thee go with *me*," Enoch taunted. "Not likely Jonathan would let thee borrow his horse." Deborah nodded her agreement.

"Why would I trust either of thee with my horse and wagon?" Pa asked.

"Thee let me drive a load to Philadelphia alone, and on this trip there would be a whole train of wagons," I said. "Pa, how can I prove myself without such a chance?"

"And what would thee do with the twelve pounds?"

I thought fast. "We'd split it evenly." Half my profit gone, but I needed that horse.

Pa waited for me to continue.

"I'd buy woodworking tools."

"Well, if Jonathan Swayne is willing to lend his horse, I suppose we could spare thee for a while. We managed well enough during thy apprenticeship, didn't we?" Then he added, "But don't come home with an empty wagon."

Until I heard those words, I hadn't realized I'd been holding my breath. Then it burst out in amazed relief. Pa was actually going to let me go. Now I could be part of showing those Indians they couldn't get by with attacking civilized people. I didn't know how that could be done without violence, but I was too excited about the coming adventure to worry about details.

Ma shook her head in resignation. I knew she was relieved that two of us were going, because we would look out for each other.

Pa folded his spectacles and put them away with the newspaper. I tried hard not to show how smug I felt. What a great adventure I was about to have! It almost made up for not getting a journeyman job right away. This way I could do something about stopping those awful attacks on settlers, see the world, or a different part of it leastways, and earn money for tools.

That night Ben hopscotched silver squares of moonlight on the floor of our bedroom as we shimmied out of our breeches and hung them on wall pegs. He said, "I wish I could go with thee, brother."

"I'd rather have thee than Enoch for a traveling partner any day. He always acts as if he's just eaten a sour apple. Pa can spare but one of us, though, and thee *is* rather young."

"Thee will see soldiers, maybe Indians and Frenchmen, maybe even a battle."

"I hope so. Someone has to keep them from killing people. I wish the Meeting would allow us to fight. But maybe there's a way to stop violence without adding to it."

Ben curled up like a puppy on our rope-strung bed, his chin resting on his hand. We were buddies as well as brothers. Joking with Ben had made dull days nearly bearable. I would do anything to defend him, I told myself, Quaker or not.

CHAPTER 2

The First Day

(May 29, 1755)

I woke with panic on the morning I was to leave. Had I overslept? Had I missed the wagon train to Wills's Creek? As I pulled on my pants, hopping on one foot, I glanced out the window. The sun was not yet peeking over the apple orchard. Relieved, I pulled my shirt on over my head. Robins and cardinals chorused, and crows yelled, "Hawk! Hawk!" to each other. Pink and gold clouds billowed in the south. Through the open window, I could smell Ma's first roses of the year, the climbing ones over the front door. A great day for a trip!

The whole family came to the barnyard to see us off. While Enoch hitched Jonathan Swayne's horse with the mulish temperament to one side of the wagon tongue, I fastened skittish Hope to the other. The horses, not yet a team, strained and neighed so much that we could scarcely control them. I tried soothing them, but Enoch scolded, "Hold thy tongue! I'll manage them my way."

Pa chuckled. "By the time they reach Philadelphia, they will know if they can pull together."

"Does thee mean the horses or the brothers?" Ma teased.

Will helped Pa stow extra tackle and a toolbox under

the buckboard, along with a canvas tarp big enough to cover the wagon. The tarp was a good idea, one I might not have thought of myself.

As we hoisted ourselves from the hubs of the wheels to the buckboard, Enoch was quick to grab the reins. Any other time, I might have resented his taking charge, but I was so glad to be setting out that I didn't take offense.

Before Enoch could even flick the whip on the horses' backs, Ma and Sheba handed up a covered basket. "Here's some bread, a wheel of cheese, and dried apples," Ma said. "I know thee will be fed along the way, but this is extra, to remind thee of home. Be careful now, and take care of each other."

"Yes, Ma, we will," I promised, trying not to roll my eyes at Ben.

"Don't come home with an empty wagon," Pa called. His voice sounded distant, but his words would accompany us on the whole trip.

Ben ran down the lane after us, waving goodbye until we outdistanced him at the end of the snake fence.

As we turned onto the Lancaster Road toward Philadelphia, I said to Enoch, "Seems odd to start a trip west by going east, doesn't it?"

"Aye," he said.

"I wonder why we have to meet the rest of the wagon train in Philadelphia. Couldn't we join them as they came through here?"

"Don't know."

"I guess everyone picks up their load in one place to start with, and mayhap there will be instructions."

"Could be."

How could he be so unconcerned when my stomach

felt like the inside of Ma's butter churn? I knew each curve of the road, but somehow everything looked new and fresh that morning. Who could guess how this trip would change my life?

Other drovers joined us along the way. Would they be part of our wagon train, too? I looked them over more carefully than usual. Most were hauling garden crops—peas, early carrots, strawberries—to the farmers' market in the city. Not likely they would be joining. But the heavy conestoga wagons might. I couldn't tell what they were carrying under those billowing tarps stretched over arched ribs. Teams of six horses pulled these huge wagons. Five of each team sported a hoop of noisy iron bells above their collars. The drover rode the sixth horse, the lead horse on the left. Another man, very strong, rode the buckboard, ready to brake the wagon on downhill slopes by pulling a lever as thick as his leg against the front wheel. These conestogas dwarfed our old wagon rattling along behind two mismatched horses.

The rutted road stretched out like a rumpled brown strap trailing over hills into valleys. We forded one narrow stream after another where the water was low enough. When the sun cleared the top of the trees and slanted into our faces, I tried speaking to Enoch again. "I'd be glad to spell thee if thee is tired."

"Nay, I'm fine."

"I could drive the horses and thee could stretch out in the wagon."

Enoch shook his head and seemed to grip the reins more tightly.

Fine. All the thoughts buzzing between my ears were far more interesting than conversation with Enoch!

The sun was high when we reached Philadelphia. What a noisy place! Vendors with heavy baskets wandered the broad cobblestone streets, shouting their wares. Barking dogs dodged hooves and wheels. The clatter and bang of construction and manufacture were everywhere. The city seemed to grow before my eyes.

There were smells, too: fresh bread from bakeries, the separate stinks of pigs and cattle herded to city butchers, and rancid fat from chandlers' shops where apprentices boiled down tallow to make candles or soap. The smell of fresh-cut wood tickled my nose. How I longed to be a cabinetmaker in the city!

At home in Chester County, everyone looked pretty much alike—English or German farm families who considered themselves lucky to have a couple of changes of homespun clothing. But here in Philadelphia I saw gentlemen in silken hose with satin breeches and fancy waistcoats. And they were wearing wigs! Women, too, wore wigs or powdered their hair to look like wigs. I saw them in their silk dresses and lacy gloves, poking their heads out of sedan chairs.

There were several Negroes, some free, others slaves. Of course, there were ordinary workmen, too, clomping around in wooden clogs and wearing coarsely woven shirts over buckskin or patched linen pants.

I stiffened when I spotted an Indian in the crowd. Was he one of the band that attacked settlers in the Back Counties? He didn't look like a murderer. He was aloof and dignified, his bronze skin gleaming in the sun. But I wasn't convinced he was innocent. Anyway, Indians were about to meet General Braddock's army, and then they would find out they couldn't get by with killing settlers.

We passed great houses with walled gardens and then neighborhoods of row houses. How would it feel to live that close to other families, with a busy street just outside the front window? Seemed like life would just crowd right in.

Finally we came to Water Street. Warehouses stood near wharves jutting out into the wide Delaware River. Large ships from England, the Low Countries, Spain, and the West Indies were docked alongside sloops from Charles Town, New York, and Boston. Bobbing in the river current, all those vessels seemed to fill the entire harbor. I gawked at their bare masts rocking crazily against the sky. All that motion made me suddenly dizzy.

The landing itself seemed to move. Wagons, carriages, handcarts, and sedan chairs milled around noisily. Clerks checked inventories against lading lists, relatives greeted returning voyagers, and vendors sold their wares among the crowd.

A man dressed in buckskin rode up to our wagon. He looked out of place in the city. His eyes seemed to take in everything at once. "Are you here for the wagon train to Wills's Creek?" he asked.

"Aye, we are," Enoch responded.

"Good. I'm Jedediah Russell, the wagon master. Move your wagon over to that warehouse where you see all those barrels, where the other wagons are headed."

Putting his index finger and thumb to his lips, Jedediah gave out a piercing whistle. When he had everyone's attention, he hollered, "While longshoremen load your wagons, come have dinner at the Three Ships

Tavern across the street. I'll give instructions as you eat, and then we'll set out."

We left our wagon at the warehouse, followed the rest of the men into the tavern, and found seats near the door. I had never been to a tavern in the city before. Ma had always packed my lunch. I studied the low-ceilinged, smoky room with small, dirty windowpanes. Ma would have a fit about the cobwebs stringing from the wagon wheel of lanterns overhead. Serving girls clutched as many tankards of foaming ale or hard cider in each hand as they could manage and sloshed them onto the dark tabletops. They joked with the men as they plunked wooden trenchers of stew and penny loaves of bread before them.

I was shocked by the boldness of these girls. They seemed to deliberately brush against men as they served them. One of them thrust herself between Enoch and me as she delivered our trenchers. I drew back as fast as I could, but she murmured, "Hello, sweetheart," right into my ear. "First time in the city?" she breathed.

I could feel blood rising in my face like bubbles in the tankards of ale.

The girl guffawed and slapped my shoulder.

"Keep thy gaze upon thy food," Enoch growled at me.

I was too mortified to look at anything else.

Jedediah, the wagon master, paced behind the tables as he gave instructions. "Welcome to each of you, and thanks for making this trip to Fort Cumberland. We have wheelwrights and carpenters to repair any damage to your wagons, a sutler to sell extra supplies along the way, drovers with a herd of cattle for the fort, and strings of packhorses carrying extra feed."

He continued, "We have to carry enough feed for our own horses to get us there and back. The first few nights we'll stop at farms where we can pasture them, but after York we'll be in wilderness where there is nothing for horses and cattle to graze on. York is about halfway between here and Wills's Creek, the easy half of our journey."

On to York! I thought, squirming with excitement.

"It's important to stay together," Jedediah went on. "This late in spring, all the trees are leafed out, so it's nigh impossible to spot redskins in the woods. The farther west we go, the worse the roads are. In fact, woodcutters are out there even now, widening the road. As they do, brush piles grow higher and offer savages a chance sneak up on us. All these wagons and livestock will make enough noise that we won't be able to hear small warning sounds."

I saw worried looks on several faces, but I wasn't afraid. This would be an exciting adventure.

"We have scouts traveling with us," Jedediah said, "but stay alert at all times. If anyone has a problem, the entire train will stop in close formation, guns at ready, because stragglers make easy targets for attacks."

That was when I began to realize that things might turn violent on this trip. I hadn't bargained for that. But too late to worry at this point.

"We'll set out as soon as the longshoremen have loaded the wagons," Jedediah continued. "We'll spend tonight at the White Horse Inn, the westernmost inn in Chester County. If we're lucky, we should reach Fort Cumberland in less than two weeks. Now finish your dinners and get back to your wagons."

We found our wagon loaded with watertight barrels of raisins, molasses, and grains. The tarp, made of several strips of canvas sewn together and waterproofed with beeswax, covered the entire load.

There were other farm wagons like ours, but the heavy conestogas dominated all of them. I could feel the hot breath of the six Belgian chunk horses next to us.

Jedediah rode his horse among the wagons, giving instructions and answering questions. Cantering up to us, he said, "I want you lads in the middle of the train. You did bring guns and ammunition, didn't you?"

"Aye," Enoch said.

"For hunting game," I added.

"I *hope* that's all you need them for. If we're attacked, you may find yourself shooting to avoid being shot." On that ominous note, Jedediah spurred his horse and rode on to speak with other wagoners.

A man came out of one of the warehouses and hailed Jedediah. "That's Benjamin Franklin," someone said.

I craned my neck to see the man whose advertisement was changing my life. He looked like most other prosperous businessmen in Philadelphia, but he had a certain presence about him that I liked.

Franklin waved to the crowd, and everyone clustered around. "Thank you for volunteering to make this trip," he said. "General Braddock was furious with Virginians for not stepping forward with wagons and supplies. He was ready to declare war on the colonies instead of the French. I promised him that Pennsylvanians would supply his need. So you are saving us from armed conflict with the greatest military power in the world." He smiled as he spoke, but he was not joking.

"Because you have volunteered, the general has granted these passes so you can't be forced to join the militia. If something happens to your horses or wagons, you will be compensated. And when you return, your grateful government will pay you."

The whole crowd cheered. Mr. Franklin handed the passes to Jedediah, bowed to him, and then to all the wagoners. Then he waved and went back to his office.

Jedediah whistled again for attention. "Everyone in line? Then let's go!"

It was mid-afternoon when we started out, with Jedediah on his horse in the lead. The forty-one supply wagons were followed by a long line of pack horses, the sutler's wagon, a herd of cattle, and finally a gaggle of women and children strung out behind. Scouts on rangy horses brought up the rear. People lined the streets, waving and cheering. "They treat us like heroes, but we haven't done anything yet," I said to Enoch.

"Let's hope we won't need to do anything heroic," he replied grimly.

I waved back at the cheering people and had trouble sitting still. Then I remembered the lone Indian I had seen on the way into town. Was he in the crowd? I looked and looked but didn't see him. Had he slipped away to warn his tribe that a whole wagon train was coming to supply the army? Were they hiding somewhere along the way to ambush us?

Enoch and I kept mostly to ourselves, but I sneaked looks at our fellow travelers and wondered about them. Some were Germans whose speech I could barely understand. Some looked older than Pa. There seemed to be only one lad about my age, and he was alone on his wagon. Most of the smaller wagons had just one driver, so I was embarrassed to be seen with Enoch. I must look like a tag-along little brother. Unfair! Making this trip was my idea in the first place. I was sure I could have handled it alone.

We did spend the first night at The White Horse Inn, only a few miles from our farm. Some of the wagoners were crowded into rooms above the tavern, three or four to a bed. Enoch and I slept under our wagon. Why pay good money to share a bed with strangers?

"I could have spent this night at home," Enoch grumbled.

"Thee may *stay* at home if thee likes. I can take the wagon to Wills's Creek myself," I offered quickly.

"Nay, Pa trusts *me* to be responsible both for the wagon and for thee."

"I can take care the wagon and myself. Go home to thy wife."

"I'd lose my share of the twelve pounds. Why do you think I'm making this trip?"

I said no more, but I wondered for the first time why Pa had let me go. Enoch could have managed alone and kept the whole twelve pounds himself. Surely Pa could have used me on the farm these weeks. Well, Pa's ways, like God's, were mysterious, but I was grateful to both of them for the opportunity to make this trip.

CHAPTER 3

The Edge of the West

Next day the road took us into a gloomy green forest. Giant trees locked their boughs overhead, shutting out the sun. In this dim light, saplings shot upwards, mayhap as high as our house, before putting out branches. Last year's fallen leaves crunched under our wagon wheels.

Footpaths crisscrossed the forest. Jedediah said they were Indian trails and our road had begun as just such a path, but since English and Germans had come to Penn's Woods, settlers' traffic had widened it from a path to a road.

The wagon train made plenty of racket riding through the woods. I wondered whether Indians were tracking us. I shivered with excitement. This sure beat plowing.

Then, all at once, we were in cleared farmland again, Lancaster County, settled by Germans. By early afternoon, we reached the town of Lancaster. "Look how neat and spotless everything looks," I said to Enoch.

"Cleanliness is next to godliness."

"Not *second* to godliness, but side by side, from the looks of this town!"

Jedediah led the wagon train to an inn for a midday dinner. I was more than ready for a break. The innkeeper must have known a big crowd was coming, because he had set up extra tables under a huge chestnut tree. We hurried to get a seat inside.

I was amazed at the beautiful woodwork in the inn. Sunlight sparkled through the mullioned windows, and beveled wood paneling covered the walls.

"I learned how to bevel wood in my apprenticeship," I whispered to Enoch.

The inn was like a catalog of the things I had been trained to make. A stairway with turned spindles and a carved banister filled one side of the room. The walnut newel post at the foot of the stairs supported a perfectly shaped ball. I longed for my own set of tools so I could find work as a journeyman. This trip would buy some of them.

Unlike the girls at the Three Ships Tavern in Philadelphia, the serving women here were motherly, modest in manner. They urged us to eat what they called *schweinshaxen.* I'd never tasted pork knuckles with sauerkraut before, but after the first taste, I wolfed it down. Then came hot apple dumplings swimming in sweet cream.

When we set out again, the afternoon sun beat down on us. I propped my feet up, pulled my hat low over my face, and leaned back against the buckboard. Mile after mile we clopped along in a gritty haze, raising dust and swatting horse flies. If I hadn't left home, I'd be cutting hay with Ben. We'd be splashing each other with creek water to cool off. Oh, well, bouncing behind a team of horses at least created a breeze.

Even though the road rose and fell over gently rolling hills, I had a sense that the land was sloping down.

Then, all of a sudden, we came to a clearing overlooking a wide, tumbling river.

I jumped to my feet and waved my hat. "The Susquehanna River! The edge of the West!" I shouted.

Enoch tried to act as if he didn't know me.

"Look!" I insisted. "There's a whole village down there by the river. Who ever expected to see brick houses way out here in the wilderness? Look, Enoch!"

"Sit down. Hold thy tongue!"

The wagons lurched down to the bottomland. The Susquehanna was the widest river I had ever seen. I tried to imagine the Delaware River in Philadelphia at flood stage and double that width. It still wouldn't be as broad as this river. And the water was roaring! Crossing it tomorrow would be . . . I didn't know the right word for it, but I was sure it would be my greatest adventure yet.

Three or four flatboats, a few rafts, and several canoes were dragged ashore and inverted well above the rushing water. I could barely make out a clearing on the other side of the river with more boats and a few buildings. All of this was Wright's Ferry.

People came running out of houses and shops to greet us. After speaking to the man in charge, Jedediah announced, "We'll camp in Mr. Wright's fallow field tonight and cross the river tomorrow. You'll sleep under your wagons, so unhitch your horses and let them graze. You'll find places to build cooking fires, and you can draw all the water you need from the river. Mr. Wright says it won't go dry!" He and Mr. Wright laughed and slapped each other on the shoulder.

We pulled our wagon into the pasture and freed the horses. Enoch sent me to the fencerow to collect firewood while he made camp for the evening. I stacked my arms full of good dry logs and kindling and balanced the load with my chin.

"Thee carries a mighty load, Friend," said a cheerful voice behind me.

I spun around, spilling some kindling. There was a short, plainly dressed Quaker woman who looked older than Ma. She laughed and helped me pick up the fallen sticks.

"I'm Susannah Wright," she said. "Welcome to Wright's Ferry. We've been expecting thy wagon train since we received Benjamin Franklin's letter."

"Good day, Friend. I'm Noble Butler, from Chester County. I am surprised to see such a town out here so far from civilization."

"Oh, we've lived here near on to twenty years now."

"Does thee feel safe? We've heard Indians are attacking settlers."

She shook her head. "The Indians are our friends. Without their help, we could not have settled here. They have been more than kind to us. Some attend our Quaker Meeting."

I raised my eyebrows. I had never heard of Indians being Quakers. "But with all the attacks in these Back Counties, can thee still trust them?"

"When thee lives with people twenty years, does business with them, sees their children grow and marry, thee builds bonds of friendship strong enough to rely on. We have no fear of Indians at Wright's Ferry. Rather, we fear *for* them. Lately, vengeful men who don't care which particular Indian offended them are the biggest danger."

So there still were some peaceful Indians. I'd never thought about that before. I remembered my manners enough to thank her for her hospitality and bid her good day again. As I carried my load of firewood back to the wagon, I wondered what would happen to those peaceful Indians when General Braddock's army encountered them. How could anybody tell which were which?

That evening Mr. Wright's field was dotted with glowing campfires. Some of the wagoners shared suppers, but we kept to ourselves, true to our upbringing. Jedediah made the rounds of each campsite, checking on gear, answering questions.

As glowing embers died and hovering lightning bugs began to flicker, all of us settled in for the night. Enoch and I stretched out on bedrolls under the wagon. I listened to the drone of locusts, the barumph of bullfrogs, and the monotonous three notes of the whippoorwill. Underneath it all, I could hear the rush of the river.

What would it be like to cross that river tomorrow? What lay on the opposite side?

CHAPTER 4

Crossing the Susquehanna

At sunrise, I got my first good look at the river, the boundary between civilization and frontier. I couldn't guess how deep it might be. I could barely see the opposite shore. How would we ever get the entire wagon train across?

Jedediah gave his two-fingered whistle to get everyone's attention. When we gathered around, he announced, "Pay attention to Mr. Wright. Your lives depend on doing exactly what he says."

James Wright raised his voice. "Here's the plan," he began. "Each ferryboat can carry one team and wagon at a time. Lead your team to the prow and tie them to the rail. Chunk the wagon wheels for stability and then soothe your horses through the crossing. Horses tend to get spooked on boats. We'll pole you across. On the other side, pull the wagon to where you will camp tonight, and turn the horses into the pasture."

"The packhorses' loads go alongside the wagons," Jedediah said. "Packhorses and cattle will swim across. Walkers will cross in canoes or johnboats. It will take all day to get everyone across, so just stay in line and wait your turn."

James Wright helped the first wagoner guide his nervous horses onto the boat and lead them to the prow. He spoke softly to the horses as he tied them. Then he took his place at the prow on the downstream side, and one of his crew stood in the middle of the boat. They set long poles into the river and walked them back toward the stern, moving the ferry out into the river current. When the first man reached the stern, he raised his pole and walked past James Wright back to the prow. Mr. Wright did the same when he reached the stern.

The rest of us watched intently. We could see horses struggling to keep their balance, and that made the boat rock even more. I could hear them neighing until they were half way across.

About that point, the boat passed the incoming second ferry with its two-man crew. When it docked, the second wagon and team were loaded and then followed the first back to the far side.

Finally we saw the first team and wagon being led up the far bank to pasture. Everybody cheered with relief for them. That boat began its slow return. Some of the walkers set out in canoes and johnboats.

After several crossings, the boatmen took a break so the livestock could swim across. Everyone had already unloaded the packhorses, and now the scouts herded horses and cattle into the river. I ran to the edge to watch.

At the bank, the animals balked, bellowing and neighing. It took a lot of whip cracking to force them into the rushing water. They churned their way across, tossing their heads and rolling their eyes, dodging driftwood and each other's horns. When a few lost their footing and were swept downstream, scouts chased after them. Finally the herd clambered up the far bank.

I was so busy watching all this that I was surprised when it was our turn to cross. Enoch tied the team to the prow and lashed the wagon to the guardrail. He held on to one horse, and I held on to the other. Our small wagon left plenty of room for loading packs from the packhorses. Then the two ferrymen pushed off into the river. I felt the swift current catch the boat. Foaming white water spilled onto the deck and drenched our feet. The wagon lurched from side to side in spite of Enoch's knots. With one hand, I clung to Hope's bridle, and with the other I clutched the side rail, half afraid to breathe.

Suddenly one of the ferrymen shouted, "Mind the driftwood! Grab a pole!"

A huge log was heading straight for us. Enoch leapt over packs and grabbed a pole. Just in time he jammed and twisted it enough to turn the log. It struck the boat sideways with a great thump, skidded off the stern, and bobbed on downstream.

"Good work," called the ferryman. "That one nearly got us. Little logs are no problem, but that one could have sunk us!"

Midstream, as we passed below a broad, forested island, the current suddenly changed. Enoch and I nearly lost our footing. No sooner had we regained our balance than we were back into the swift flow and had to struggle once more. The ferrymen avoided rocks, pushing off against them in the very nick of time.

I was just beginning to enjoy the cool spray and anticipate the rhythm of the boat's rocking when we reached the western bank. I felt a little disappointed as we untied the team and led them up to pasture.

On this side, there was nothing to do but wait for the other wagons. Women traveling with their husbands set up their tents and tried to make them homey. Two kinds of women were traveling without men. One group stayed together, keeping to themselves. Others offered their services to wagoners without wives. I tried to watch without being obvious, but Enoch elbowed me and muttered, "Mind thy own business."

So I wandered over to the edge of the pasture and straddled a fallen log. I was just sitting there picking at the loose bark when a curly-haired girl with a round face perched herself just in front of me. She grinned a gap-toothed grin.

"Didn't mean to make ye jump," she apologized. "Just looked like ye've found a prime place to sit, and thought I'd join ye, iffen ye don't mind, that is?" It wasn't a question, but her voice rose as if it were.

"N-no," I stuttered. "Thee is welcome to sit here, of course."

"Ye look like a safe enough person to talk to. I don't trust some of the men, and the women all seem to have their own ways, which are none of mine."

"I suppose not," I said, trying to sound unconcerned.

"Aye, some of the women are with their men, and some are lookin' for a man. Not me! I'm goin' to meet my man at Wills's Creek."

"Thy husband is a soldier there?" I asked, in spite of myself.

"Not my husband, my man. He'll be my husband

someday, I trust. But for now, the important thing is not to be lost from each other. So I've come to find him."

"Thee left thy family and came all this way to find thy soldier?"

"Not me family! They all died back in the Old Country, so I indentured meself to come to Pennsylvania. I hoped to find a rich husband, but me master instead is quite married and not quite rich. Then I met Charley, a soldier young and handsome with a promisin' future, and we fell in love. When his orders came for Fort Cumberland, he had no time even to say goodbye! He marched off with the others, leavin' me heartbroken behind. So when I learned of this wagon train goin' to the very place where Charley is, I says to meself, 'Here's yer chance, Molly, and yer not like to find a better one.' Me mistress gave me money and sent me to the wharf to buy cloth from the merchants, and I just attached meself to the wagon train and forgot her errand!" She grinned again, obviously pleased with herself.

I stared at her. Molly was a thief, a runaway indentured servant chasing after a soldier who was not her husband. I didn't know what to say.

Molly, however, felt no loss for words. "And why did ye come?"

I felt the hairs on the back of my neck start to rise. Ma and Pa had taught me to keep my business to myself. Yet Molly had been so open that I felt obliged to respond. So I stammered, "It was a chance to help settlers in trouble."

Not "to teach Indians a lesson" or "to earn twelve pounds" or "to have a great adventure." I don't know why I said that. I didn't know how to talk to girls.

"Aye, I could tell ye were a helper. It's written in yer face. A good face ye have, sir. And would ye be willin' to help me?"

"What kind of help does thee need?" I asked cautiously.

"Why, none at the moment, but on a trip like this, a girl can never tell. There might be an Indian attack, one of these wagoners might pester me, I might even get tired of walkin' and need a ride. . . ?" Again, her voice made a question of what was only a statement. She seemed to inch closer. "I can tell ye are a Friend. Will ye be me friend upon this trip to Wills's Creek?"

"Of course I would come to thy aid," I said. Then I stopped short.

"And will ye be me friend upon this trip to Wills's Creek?" she repeated softly, insistently.

To my great relief, Enoch cut in. "Noble! Give me a hand with this barrel."

"Ah, yer name is Noble, is it?" Molly murmured. "A fine name, me friend. I'll see ye later." And she scooted off the log and disappeared among the women.

"What was thee doing, talking to that girl?" Enoch demanded.

"I wasn't. She was doing all the talking. Enoch, she's a runaway indentured servant trying to catch up with a soldier at Fort Cumberland!"

"Keep to thyself. Don't get caught up with trollops."

"But she asked for my help."

"Thee is the one needing help. Stay away from girls on this trip, Noble. I promised Ma I'd look after thee."

I helped Enoch with the barrel and then went back to

my log. I was glad Enoch had interrupted, and I was glad Molly had left.

She made me feel the same way as when the serving girl in the Philadelphia tavern brushed against me, all hot and confused. But Molly didn't tease me. She trusted me with her life story. She must think me manly enough because she asked for my help.

How could I help her? I couldn't even offer her a ride on the buckboard because Enoch had already decided she was a trollop. But she trusted me, and she was all alone. Ma would want me to look after her, surely.

I worried about it a little longer, but it was too big a conundrum to solve in one day.

Ma and Pa had taught us it was rude to ask others what they were up to. It was none of our concern, and what we were doing was nobody else's business. But on this trip, surely that lesson didn't apply. We were all strangers to each other, but our business was the same, delivering supplies to General Braddock. Would it be wrong to find out who people were and where they were from? From the time we set out from Philadelphia, I began learning their names, their first names, mainly.

There was that one lad about my age traveling alone in the wagon just ahead of ours. When evening came and the wagons were circled tightly, it made sense to share a cooking fire with him. I learned he was Peter, the son of a widowed farmer, and he came from Bucks County. After supper, he and I began to talk, sitting crosslegged, poking the fire with sticks and watching sparks spiral to the stars above.

"From here on, I guess we're in Indian territory," I said.

"My pa dislikes savages, and he really hates the French for corrupting them. We've heard lots of stories about settlers being attacked," Peter said.

"We have, too. Does thee know anyone who's been attacked?" I wondered if Enoch would fault me for asking a personal question like that, but he just smoked his pipe and seemed to ignore us.

"Do you mean settlers or soldiers?"

"I meant settlers. Does thee know soldiers?"

"Two of my brothers have moved from home. Jacob went to New York to farm. He wrote us that Senecas attacked his neighbor as he mowed hay. Jacob found him with a tomahawk between his shoulder blades. The savages stole two of the older children and killed the baby with its mother."

I shuddered.

"Jacob told Pa the sight of this family murdered by heathen made him join the militia," Peter continued. "He doesn't have his own family yet, and he felt duty-bound to go protect the colony for a while. Another brother, Lemuel, moved to Virginia and joined Colonel Washington's militia."

"Mayhap thee will see him at Fort Cumberland."

"Nay, I won't be seeing Lemuel. He died in a skirmish with the French and the redskins two months ago."

"Oh!" I caught my breath. "Oh, I'm sorry."

"He died for a good cause. Pa says we lived well enough with the tribes until the French butted in. He says we must send the French back to France and push the savages beyond the Forks of the Ohio. Only then can we have peace."

"Send the French back to France and push the savages

beyond the Forks of the Ohio," I repeated. "That's right! We have to show them they can't get by with killing."

"My other brothers are helping Pa on the farm," Peter went on. "But Pa felt it his duty to send me on this trip to Wills's Creek. He said since our stuffy old Quaker Assembly won't protect the frontier, this is the least we could do."

Enoch and I exchanged glances. The leaders of the Assembly were weighty Quakers, just trying to live up to William Penn's vision. Pa would have had something to say, but I didn't feel ready to defend the Assembly. Apparently Enoch didn't, either.

"And why did you two come?" Peter asked.

Enoch cut in, "To earn twelve pounds." He probably feared I might say as much about our family as Peter had told about his.

Daniel, whose wagon followed ours, must have been listening. He called out, "Aye, that's the way with you Quakers! You won't fight, but you'll make money."

Enoch clenched his jaw and said nothing. But I couldn't let that pass.

"It's not just the money!" I said. "Friends don't believe in fighting, but we want to teach those Indians a lesson, too. This supply trip is something we can do in good conscience, and that's why we came."

"That may be *why you* came, young man, but your brother, here, he came to make money, and that's why your pa let you come, too," Daniel replied. "After you see what's going on, you'll be ready to take up arms yourself. We should force the whole Quaker Assembly to make this trip! Then maybe they'd wake up."

Jedediah's calm deep voice rang out. "Call it a day. No more talk tonight."

I felt corked up. I was convinced Jedediah had interrupted only because Daniel butted in and tried to start an argument. Daniel sure had it in for Quakers.

That bothered me. Oh, I had my own questions about Quaker rules, and Pa and I had had some lively discussions about them. But Daniel had it all wrong. Friends in the Assembly don't vote money for war because we believe there are better ways to solve disagreements. We *are* careful with money, but money isn't what we think of mostly.

Besides, Daniel was lumping all of us together. He didn't care whether Enoch and I thought differently from the weighty Quakers about anything. And when I tried to tell him, he wouldn't listen. He seemed to dislike us just because we were Quakers. How unfair! Did all the wagoners think like Daniel?

Sprawled under our wagon, I whispered to Enoch, "Is that why no one has been very friendly with us? Because we're Friends?"

"Thee heard Jedediah: no more talk tonight," Enoch answered.

Then I remembered. Some people *had* been friendly. Peter. And Molly.

CHAPTER 5
Storm

After passing through York the next day, we were truly in wilderness. The trail was narrower than before. I felt hemmed in and a little spooked. Wilderness was full of hidden dangers. It was too easy to trip over roots, get knocked in the head by low hanging branches, or be ambushed by savages in hiding. And no wonder Indians were savage! There was nothing out here to make people more than animals. I could see why settlers couldn't wait to make clearings. Space makes people feel more secure, I suppose.

Yet wilderness has its own beauty. Spears of sunlight pierced the gloom. Bird song filled the air. Squirrels jumped from tree to tree as horses plodded beneath them. Deer flashed their white rumps and vanished into dense thickets. Except for the trail itself, there were no signs that anyone had ever been through here.

Just north of the Pigeon Hills, we began hearing a strange rustling in the woods. The trees and even the ground itself seemed constantly in motion. "Passenger pigeons," Jedediah explained as he cantered past our wagon.

"Look! There must be millions of them," I said to Enoch.

Shoulder to shoulder, the birds were pecking and turning over last year's leaves, looking for beech nuts and acorns. The ones at the back, finding no more food, flew ahead. They were a gigantic roller, gleaning the forest floor. In the trees, more pigeons crowded each other off upper limbs, arguing among themselves in a rattling, musical way.

Every once in a while a branch would give under their weight and come crashing down. Then all the birds in that tree took flight at once, making a huge roar.

The train slowed to a stop, everyone spellbound.

"Look at that!"

"I never saw so many birds!"

And then someone called, "Fresh meat for supper!"

That did it. Yelling and whooping, wagoners began clubbing the pigeons and stuffing them, still writhing, into burlap bags. Blood and commotion surrounded us.

I couldn't stand it. The frenzy of the men, the frantic birds crashing into each other, blood and feathers splattering everywhere, sent me nearly beside myself. The pigeons were beautiful birds, almost as big as pullets, and their feathers had wondrous changeable colors. Their strange red eyes filled with terror. I was feeling their panic.

"Stop! Stop it!" I hollered at Enoch. "What is thee doing?"

"Fresh meat," Enoch yelled, without stopping. "Don't just stand there. Pick 'em up and put 'em in the wagon." He gripped the muzzle of the gun in both hands and swung the stock in wide circles through the swarm of fleeing pigeons.

"Stop, I say! We'll never eat that many before they spoil. Enoch, please!"

"Hold thy tongue and stay out of my way!"

I climbed back up onto the buckboard and clamped my hands over my ears. I squeezed my eyes shut. I was sickened by globs of blood and clinging feathers. I couldn't believe that civilized people could act that way.

Jedediah cracked his whip in the air to cut through the orgy of pigeon slaughter. He whistled and yelled until he got everyone's attention. Finally the wagoners wiped their bloody hands on their pants and climbed back up to their seats on the wagons.

Jedediah held up the train until everyone had quieted. Then he said sternly, "Never get sidetracked like that again. In all the ruckus, Indians could have ambushed us, and we would have been pigeons ourselves. We were lucky this time, but if you get carried away like that again, your pigeon suppers may be your last meal!"

Abashed, the wagoners began to move the wagons. Hardly anyone spoke.

But Enoch taunted me. "Thee grew up on a farm, even killed chickens thyself. Why did a little pigeon blood upset thee?"

"A *little* pigeon blood? Thee was like a fox in a chicken house, Enoch, thee and everyone else, savages, killing as many as thee could. What got into thee?"

"Thee is a lily-livered coward. What will thee do if we encounter Indians?"

I had no answer.

The horses were restless after all that excitement, and blood and bird droppings made the trail sticky. Crews of woodcutters had recently widened it to nearly twelve feet. They had cut the trees but left stumps high enough to catch an axle or break a wheel. Even on this widened road, wagons could barely get through. Enoch steered the team with great care. It was hard to miss all the rocks in the road. The train plodded slowly. No one wanted a wagon overturned.

I still felt jangled by the pigeon slaughter. There were thick walls of felled trees on either side of the road, and there might be Indians or Frenchmen hiding behind them. Even a squirrel jumping from one branch to another sounded like the beginning of an attack. All my senses were on alert.

An unexpected calm fell over the forest. No birds sang and nothing moved. The sun cast a greenish light. Horses began to whinny and step sideways. The hair on my arms stood upright and my scalp prickled.

Suddenly the sky turned dark and the wind picked up, whipping branches and sending dust devils swirling on the trail ahead. Lightning flashed and thunder boomed at exactly the same time! Walnut-sized hail hammered the forest, stripping leaves from trees and piling up in glistening mounds. Was God punishing us for killing all those pigeons?

The horses reared wildly. All of us jumped from our wagons and ran to catch the bridles. Curtains of rain swept in waves down the trail toward us. A blinding flash struck a maple just off the trail. It exploded away from its roots and left a steaming stump boiling with sap. The tree landed upright against two others, swayed dizzily, then fell with a crash that shook the ground, taking other trees and large branches down with it.

Horses tried to bolt, their eyes rolling, their manes almost erect, their tails bushy. Rain streamed down our faces as we slipped and slid, trying to control our teams.

I clung to the bridles of our rearing horses, trying to avoid their hooves clawing the air as they swung me off my feet. I shouted but could scarce hear my own voice.

Trees twisted and bent in violent gusts. Broken branches seemed to fly off in all directions. Streaks of lightning stabbed the ground on every side, and thunder filled my head. Behind, I could hear bellows of livestock, screams of women and children. I remembered promising to look after Molly, but what could I do? It was more than I could manage to look after the horses.

Finally the lightning began to flash less frequently. Sharp cracks of thunder diminished to distant rumbles. Then a steady rain settled in. Wet clothes plastered us as we waded ankle deep in mud churned up by the horses.

Jedediah slogged from wagon to wagon to check on everyone. No one seemed injured; no livestock had been struck by lightning. Falling branches had hit a few wagons but caused little damage. Had any of the cargo spoiled?

"We'll stay here until the road dries out," Jedediah announced. "It's too wet to sleep on the ground or build fires, so sleep in your wagons tonight."

Without campfires, no one could cook the pigeons. I thought it only right, after all. We ate cold suppers and huddled quietly in our own wagons. Scouts tethered the horses just off the road, and men took turns on guard duty throughout the night.

CHAPTER 6

Stories in the Rain

The next morning, rain still drummed steadily. Jedediah sloshed from wagon to wagon saying, "Looks like a three-day rain to me. Let's clear some of this brush for shelters. Try to find some dry wood and a place for a fire."

In no time we made a clearing and built some lean-tos facing away from the rain. A few drovers used extra canvases to cover a common cooking fire. They lashed corners to convenient trees, overlapping the edges of several tarps to leave a smoke hole in the center. Smoke curled out along the sides as well. Under this shelter, we threw wet, muddy clothes over sagging clotheslines and began cleaning and smoking the pigeons on racks around the fire.

During this forced wait, there was nothing better to do than swap stories and argue politics. Enoch and I squatted on the edge of a group around the central fire. Peter was there, too. Horst, a grizzled old German, was talking about life in the Old Country. His voice rose and fell with the sound of rain on the tarp over our heads.

"The lord of the manor owned us," he said. "All day we tended his crops, no time for our own garden. Many winters nearly we starved, because harvest went to the master, little left for us. If we hunted game in his woods, it was a crime."

Horst's voice rose. "He decided jobs for our sons, and he could have our women any time he wanted. Everything belonged to him. And when the call came to fight, he would send *us*. Not our war, *his*! Yet we had to fight and die for his reasons.

"Ach! It was not easy! We hid every coin. If the master knew we had money, he would take it to pay his debts. Finally came another call to war. He wanted to take me and mein boys, leaving mein frau and daughters mit no protection. So one dark night we ran away, took what little we had mit us."

He continued, "We traveled nights, hiding days, nearly starving. At Hamburg, we had no money to pay passage, but captain said anyway we could sail. 'Indenture yourselves when we land at Philadelphia,' he told us.

"What could I say? Well, jah," he allowed ruefully, "I could have asked more questions. Who knew we would be indentured each to a different master?"

"Were you together on the ship?" Peter asked.

"Nein. Men and boys in one cabin, women and girls in another. Nearly we starved. Captain didn't feed us, and we had little food of our own. Some passengers were willing to share. Gott bless them! Then the fever struck, and mein daughters died."

Horst paused, overcome with grief. Everyone stared into the fire.

"In Philadelphia, the indenture broker was waiting for us. We had no skills but farming, so our indentures was long. Mein frau was taken as cook by one family and I as farm worker miles from her. Mein two boys went to other farms, not together. So our happiest day turned to sorrow."

Horst mopped his face in the light of the flickering fire. Then he brightened a bit. "But mein indenture is over. Then I worked to free mein frau. Now we work to free our sons. The twelve pounds from this trip will do it. Then we begin buying land for ourselves. Freedom and opportunity!"

Steady rain still drummed on the canvas. I had forgotten where we were, listening to Horst's story. I started to get up, but Daniel spoke next, so I settled in again.

"Aye, freedom and opportunity!" he exclaimed. His lip was curled in a smile we all knew he didn't mean. "You're right, Horst, we have freedom and opportunity. But we could have more if the Proprietors would loose their hold on the land. And we could protect what we have if those mealy-mouthed Quakers would let us!"

Mealy-mouthed? Is that what people called Quakers? Why would they think Quakers mealy-mouthed?

Enoch relighted his pipe.

"Proprietors? Who are they?" Horst asked.

Daniel leaned forward to explain. "When William Penn died, his sons, the Proprietors, inherited all the unsettled land that King Charles had given their father. But they don't live here. They pay an agent to collect rents and sell land to settlers. The agent also negotiates with redskins to purchase more land. But the Proprietors have told him that no matter what the Assembly votes, the Penns and their properties are never to be taxed. If the agent acts against their interests, he's out of a job."

"Sounds like manor lords in mein old country," Horst said.

"Is the agent fair with the tribes?" I asked. Enoch elbowed me, but I ignored him.

"Not really," Daniel replied. "He gets them drunk and then talks them into land sales that nobody sober would agree to. But the stupid savages still believe William Penn's promises. When they think the agent is unfair, they complain to the governor. The governor always meets with them and gives them gifts of trade goods."

"So after they complain, they get more than the agents offered. Sounds fair enough to me," Molly said. Several others nodded their agreement.

"Where do the French come in?" Peter asked.

"The French came in the back door, so to speak, on the St. Lawrence and Mississippi. They trade for furs all over the interior," Daniel replied. "Now they have built Fort Duquesne on the Forks of the Ohio, and they've made friends with heathen in the interior. The French and English have been fighting for years."

"We read about that in the *Pennsylvania Gazette*," I whispered to Enoch.

Daniel continued, "Now the French are telling the redskins the English are after all their land. The fools believe them."

Peter said, "The French sell them guns and ammunition, don't they? Settlers have reason to fear."

"That's right," Daniel said. "And if settlers are scared enough to come back east, then the French can take over without fighting. Of course, then the French will take the land, so the Indians are really stupid to fight for them."

"Well, there's Indians, and there's Indians," interrupted Christopher, one of the scouts, "and they're far from stupid. I've traded with 'em for years. I've even lived with 'em in their villages over a few winters."

All of us turned to look at this woodsman in buckskin pants and a coarse linen shirt. He had a scar on his cheek that could have come from a knife fight.

"Why do they kill settlers and steal women and children?" Peter asked.

"Because we've killed their people. When that happens, a tribe either kills one of us or takes someone to replace theirs that was killed. They adopt the white person and treat 'em very well. I met some of them 'prisoners' in their villages, blue-eyed Indians by the time I met them. They didn't want to go back to white folks' ways."

"Even the women?" Molly asked.

"Even the women," Christopher said.

I shook my head slowly.

"I think it goes back to the Walking Purchase of 1737," Christopher continued. "The Delaware are still sore about that."

"The Walking Purchase?" Horst asked. "What happened?"

Christopher drew a stick from the fire and sketched a rough map of eastern Pennsylvania in the dirt at his feet. "Here's the Delaware River," he pointed with his stick, "and here's Philadelphia. Up here are the Lehigh Hills and the Blue Mountains."

"That's about where our farm is!" Peter said.

"None of this was in the King's land grant to William Penn. But Penn's son Thomas, one of your Proprietors," Christopher nodded to Daniel, "'found' a copy of a deed. He claimed it was signed by Delaware chiefs and dated 1686. The original had been lost for years, Penn said, but he wanted the land described in this copy. Even though none of the chiefs had ever heard of this deed, and their memories are quite good, they honored this 'found copy.'"

"Which land?" Daniel asked.

Christopher continued, "The deed called for starting at a tree by the River Delaware here in Bucks County." His stick pointed to the map in the dirt. "From there westward up Neshaminy Creek, then along a trail northward 'as far as a man could go in a day and a half.' From that point back to the Delaware River. A man can walk about thirty miles in a day and a half, so this is what the tribe thought they were giving up." Christopher drew a small area on his map.

"But the Proprietors," he went on, "advertised for the three fastest walkers in the area. They promised five pounds and 500 acres to the man who could go the farthest in a day and a half. Then they took them over the ground ahead of time and even cleared and blazed a trail for them!

"The day of the Walk came, and folks turned out to watch. Some of the chiefs planned to walk with the three men. They started out at a reasonable pace, but pretty soon the white men began to run. The chiefs called out, 'Walk, walk, not run!' but away they went. The Delaware gave up in disgust and went home. They knew they were being cheated."

"How far did the runners go?" Peter asked.

"By sunset, they were already on the north side of the Blue Mountains up here." Christopher pointed with his stick. "By noon the next day, the only man left in the race was pretty spent. He threw himself on the ground, reached out his arm as far as he could and grabbed a sapling, and that was the furthest point. It was about sixty-five miles from where they started."

"Anyone can see that was unfair," I said.

"Yes, but that's not all. Instead of drawing the line straight east back to the Delaware River, they ran it as far *north*east, upriver, as they could. So all this area," he pointed again to his map in the dirt, "was the Walking Purchase. It's more than two and a half times what the chiefs had intended to sell. Whole tribes were cheated."

Peter studied the dirt map. "There aren't any redskins around us. Where did they go?"

"They went over the next mountains into the Wyoming Valley." Christopher had to stand to extend his stick that far on his map.

"I suppose they complained to the governor," Daniel said.

"Aye, you bet they did. The governor said he'd look into it. It was nigh twenty year ago all this happened, and the present governor is still 'looking into it.'"

I said, "What are the Delaware doing about it?"

Daniel broke in: "They're attacking settlers on the frontier, that's what they're doing. They're attacking the wrong people, but that's Indians for you. They can't tell one white man from another."

"Can you tell one Indian from another?" Christopher asked. "Most people can't. They see a redskin, think they're going to get scalped, and shoot him first. Add the French to the mix, supplyin' tribes with guns and ammunition and tellin' them the English intend to take all their land, and we've got war on the frontier."

"And a Quaker Assembly that won't fund a militia!" Daniel broke in. "How can those phony saints still think of savages as brothers when they *know* that they are murderers and thieves?"

Reuben, a quiet Quaker who had kept in the background, said, "William Penn made a promise to the Indians that still holds, even though people have violated it."

"If Quakers don't believe in fighting, that's fine with me," Daniel growled, "but they shouldn't block them that believes in meeting force with force. A government must protect its citizens. If the Quaker Party can't do that, they should step aside."

"That's exactly why the English sent General Braddock and his men over here," Jedediah said.

I jumped when he spoke. I hadn't seen him join the circle around the fire.

He continued, "The Crown has to protect her colonies in the New World. The army needs a lot of support to travel so far back into the wilderness. Since they've come to fight for us, we have to supply 'em."

"And that's why we're going to Wills's Creek," Daniel said.

"Yes, Fort Cumberland is Braddock's jumping-off point for Fort Duquesne," Jedediah replied. "The men at Fort Cumberland have little to eat but whatever game they shoot. Surrounded by Indians, they can't shoot much. So they'll be glad to see us. I hope this rain doesn't delay us too much longer."

Then he said, "Even after the rain ends, it will be a few more days before the road is dry enough to travel."

That night I listened to rain pattering on the canvas just above my head and mulled over what we had heard. "Daniel seems to blame Quakers in the Assembly for all the trouble on the frontier," I said to Enoch.

"Aye."

"Isn't it right to keep William Penn's promises?"

"So we've been taught."

"Daniel thinks it's Quakers' fault the Indians are attacking?"

"Aye."

"He thinks peaceful ways are weak and foolish."

"Um."

"And he dislikes us because we're Quakers. That's not fair!"

"Go to sleep, Noble."

I quit trying to talk to Enoch, but I couldn't quit thinking. It was easy to see why the Walking Purchase upset the Indians, and they wouldn't get over it until the governor made it right. But how could it ever be made right? Would Peter and his family have to give up their farm to settle things? What if that were our farm? I was pretty sure Pa wouldn't give it up.

Then I wondered about Christopher. He seemed to like Indians more than settlers. Could he be trusted as a scout? Might he lead us into a trap?

CHAPTER 7

Peter's Wagon

The rain pinned us down nearly a week, so I had some time to write. When I pulled the account book out of my knapsack, along with a bottle of ink, a handful of goose feathers, and a penknife for cutting quills, Enoch was pretty surprised. But he left me alone. I was glad he didn't ask why I had brought all that stuff along.

I wasn't earning or spending money, but talking with people who weren't Quakers had raised plenty of questions in my own mind about where I stood. As for what I was worth, it didn't look like much. I hadn't been able to stop Enoch from killing pigeons, I couldn't calm the horses during the storm, and I had no answers for people who didn't like Quakers. So I just wrote about where we had been and what we had seen. I filled one whole page with questions I couldn't answer.

Finally Jedediah decided he could wait no longer although the roads were barely dry.

"Today we cross South Mountain," he said. "The trail takes us over at the lowest point, but it's hardly a gap. Steer your teams to the inside of the road. We don't want to lose anybody over the edge of a cliff. This will probably be our hardest day."

Woodcutters widening the road had undercut the inside of the hills. Heavy rain brought landslides and washed out great gullies. At least now the embedded rocks that had plagued us helped us keep our footing.

The farther we went, the drier and steeper the road became. As we climbed the mountain, I could look down into the tops of trees maybe a hundred feet tall! Horses strained pulling their heavy loads. Harnesses creaked and wheels wobbled. Jedediah rode from one wagon to the next to say, "It's time to attach tow ropes to the front of your wagon. You'll need to help the horses pull," he said.

Enoch stopped and handed me the reins for the first time. "I'm stronger than thee," he said, "so I'll help the horses. Just guide them as close as thee can to the inner side of the road." He jumped down, attached our heaviest ropes to the iron hooks, looped them over his head and under one arm, and took his place in front of the horses.

I was fairly tense, but I have to say I enjoyed driving Enoch and the team. For sure, my job was easier than his. We inched our way up the mountain, hugging the cliff wall. Some of the turns were so steep that the wagon slid sideways. Enoch was yelling at me, but I couldn't answer. I was biting my lip and working hard to keep the horses going. They couldn't gain any momentum because Peter's team ahead of us kept slipping backwards.

Finally we reached the top and stopped to rest. The summit was a wide, rocky clearing with thinly scattered trees. I was awestruck by the view from up there. To the west were ranges of mountains, furry with trees. Back to the east, I could see scattered farms, looking like spots of mange on the forested flanks of hills. I tried to see the Susquehanna behind us but couldn't.

It looked as if the west was just one mountain after another. How much farther could it be to Fort Cumberland? Was Wills's Creek one of those streams I saw?

All of us stretched and groaned and told each other how tough that pull up the mountain had been. We felt like we had surely conquered the most difficult part of the road. After all, Jedediah had said this would be our hardest day. We wiped the dust off our faces and nearly drained our canteens.

Then Jedediah came around with a new set of orders. "It's time to hook your tow ropes to the back of your wagons. If you are traveling alone, be sure you have some way to brake, or else lead your team. The way down is steeper than the way up!"

We didn't realize what we were in for. Enoch moved our ropes to the iron hooks on the back of the wagon and tied them tightly together. Then he handed them to me and said, "It's my turn to ride. Pull back with all thy might. I don't like the looks of this road. I'll try driving the team, but I may have to get down and lead them. At least it isn't muddy. It looks as if it hasn't rained on this side of the mountain for weeks."

Jedediah gave the signal, and we set out. The first wagons had better traction on the sloping trail than the rest of us. We fought loose rocks and dirt after their passage.

Enoch stood with the backs of his knees braced against the buckboard. He pulled hard on the reins to check our momentum. Dust billowed uphill so we couldn't see the road. Those in front called back warnings to the rest of us.

I coughed and turned my head, but I kept breathing dust. Even tying a bandanna over my nose and mouth didn't help. Dust just roiled up beneath it. I could hardly see where we were going. Daniel's team behind us skidded, and the horses' breath was hot on my neck. Their rumps were on the road as they tried not to tumble down the trail.

Enoch, peering through the dust at Peter's wagon just ahead, saw that it was drifting too close to the edge of the cliff. "Peter! Look out!" he shouted.

Peter looked back over his shoulder. "What's the matter?"

Just then Peter's wagon wobbled suddenly and the back wheel left the road!

"Jump!" Enoch yelled.

Peter leapt from the wagon and tumbled onto the rough trail. His wagon lurched out into empty space and then toppled over, dragging the scrambling horses with it. Someone screamed. The wagon train came to a skidding halt.

Stunned, all of us watched the dizzying fall of the flimsy wagon. It bounced and splintered against the rock face of the cliff. Barrels broke open, raining grain down the mountainside. The horses somersaulted to their deaths at the bottom, where they lay sprawled like broken toys.

For an instant it seemed as if time had stopped. No one moved or spoke.

Then Peter, gray as a corpse under all that dust, scrambled to his feet and turned to Jedediah. "I'm sorry!" was all he could say.

"Son, a good thing you jumped!" Jedediah said in a

choked voice. Other wagoners crowded around Peter, clapping him on the shoulder or tousling his hair.

Jedediah collected his thoughts and then said, "Peter, you need to stick with us. It isn't safe to go back alone. You can help one of the other wagoners or join the walkers. Men, you see how you must hug the inside of the road. Let's go on, now. We can rest at the bottom."

Horst offered Peter a seat on his buckboard. Then we crept even more carefully down the trail. All of us were sobered by what had happened, knowing that could have been our wagon instead of Peter's.

Finally the road leveled. I heard the sound of water before I saw it. Just ahead, Licking Creek burbled along. The wagon train came to a halt. We all needed a rest. I gave a whoop of joy as everyone jumped from their wagons.

Road dust had caked on our sweaty faces and made sticky brownish-gray masks. When we took off our hats, little rivers of sweat trickled down our foreheads. We burst out laughing as we looked at each other. One after another, we knelt at the edge of the creek, scooped water into our hats, and dumped it over our heads to cool off. Then in playful relief, we started throwing water on each other. Women and children splashed in the stream. Peter was the only one who didn't join in.

I swam just under water out to the middle of the creek. When I surfaced, there was Molly standing on a rock right in front of me. She had tucked up her petticoat and shift so her legs were bare to her knees. Water dripped off of her curls. With a big grin, she threw water in my face, inviting me to play.

I spluttered as I shook water from my eyes. Just then,

Enoch came up behind me, knocked me off balance, and ducked me in the creek. Molly splashed off downstream, laughing. I turned to duck Enoch in turn, but he was too quick for me. He had already climbed onto the bank.

Jedediah clanged an iron bar against a pan to get our attention. "As soon as you water your horses, we need to get going again. The scouts say redskins are around."

After what we had been through, all we needed now was an ambush. A chill of fear ran through me. If I had watched for Indians before, I was even more on edge now. But we saw none.

Around the campfire that evening, Enoch and I sat next to Peter and Horst. Peter had not said a single word since the loss of his wagon and team. Finally he broke his long silence. "Pa will kill me."

"Nay," I replied, "he'll be glad thee jumped."

Horst lit his pipe with a glowing stick drawn from the campfire. Exhaling, he studied the cloud of smoke. "*Ach, mein Gott.*" He struggled for English words to express his deep feelings. "I have known many losses—crops, tools, farm, house—but the hardest thing is to lose a child. No father could value wagon and team above a son."

Jedediah emerged from the darkness behind us. "Horst is right," he said. "I've led many a train like this, and on each trip we lose a wagon or two. Sometimes an entire family is killed, or sometimes the father, leaving widow and orphans. Your instincts were right today, Peter, and you'll hear your father say so."

"Mayhap I should go back and check on the horses. Maybe they didn't die."

"No, son, there's no doubt they're dead. We saw them splayed out on the rocks, their insides broken open. There was naught to do for them."

"What about the wagon? Could any of it be recovered?"

"Give it up, Peter," Jedediah said. "Accept what happened, be grateful for every breath, and keep going. Likely we'll see worse losses before we're home."

CHAPTER 8
Massacre

The trail narrowed the next day to little more than a path. Three packhorses could hardly proceed side by side. Enoch and I were ducking and weaving to keep from being whipped by low-hanging branches. Jedediah rode back and forth the length of the train. "Close ranks," he urged. We all knew he feared an attack.

At last we reached the Potomac River and found the broad trail to Fort Cumberland that had been cut just that spring for General Braddock. He had brought powerful cannons from his ship, and the heavy caissons carrying them had carved deep ruts in the road. Here two wagons could easily pass each other. Jedediah breathed, "Whew! At last a wider road!"

Time and again, Jedediah sent Christopher and another scout ahead to look for French or Indian activity. Each time, they brought back the same news. "Settlers are scared to death. Everyone tells of an attack they've *heard* of, but nobody's actually seen one."

The farther west we went, the more we met fleeing settlers coming east with their wagons piled high. They were in such a rush that they hardly paused to talk to us. But one frightened old man chattered a continuing account as he passed the wagon train.

"They come outta the woods with whoops and chop down men in the fields, and then they race on to the cabins and kill the women and children! You could be workin' and singin', thinkin' no danger nigh, when all of a sudden yer struck! Even if ye take yer gun to the field with ye, ye have no chance. Even if ye leave a loaded gun with yer woman, it's no use! Them savages is too much. Better to leave yer crops in the ground and give up the land."

"Leave crops in the ground? What will they do this winter?" I wondered.

"If they don't leave now, they may not see winter," Enoch said.

Hearing that old man and seeing those fleeing settlers, I hated Indians. I pictured Ben and me working in the south pasture clearing fencerows. In my imagination, we saw smoke rising from the house and heard Ma and Sheba screaming. Then bloodthirsty Indians spilled out and ran toward Ben and me, tomahawks raised, yelling their heads off.

None of them could be trusted, even if they looked safe enough. I was sure Enoch and I were doing the right thing on this wagon train. The Indians must be stopped. Tamed or killed, one way or another, they must be stopped.

Then Christopher reported, "We've found a cold campfire, a broken tomahawk, tattered pieces of white people's clothing. But so far we've seen no Indians."

Jedediah circled back to speak to each of us. "Stay as close together as possible. If you see danger, fire your gun to warn everyone. We'll not stop to rest today. With luck, we'll get to Fort Cumberland by dark."

Mid-afternoon, I noticed a large number of vultures circling overhead. Must have been a lot of dead animals nearby.

Then, around a bend, we came upon a silent plantation. Smoke still curled from a burned-out cabin and barn. Jedediah held up his hand, and we slowed to a stop. In the short lane to the cabin were three crumpled bodies, probably a father and his two nearly grown sons. Their scalps were gone. Blood caked their bare skulls. A tomahawk still stuck in the back of the smaller son. All three faces were frozen in agonized fear.

Severed arms and legs of the mother and young children littered the cabin threshold. Against the stoop I saw small blond heads covered with bloody caps. Their tiny faces still held the terror of their final minutes. There were piles of charred bones on the dirt floor of the burned cabin. The torsos of the mother and little ones.

Here right in front of my eyes was what my imagination had balked at. I couldn't bring myself to see this when I pictured Indians attacking Ben and me in the south pasture. Yet this was real, far worse than anything I had imagined.

Suddenly I realized why the vultures had come. All I had eaten that day came roaring up my throat, and I vomited over the side of the wagon. Shaking all over, I lifted my head sheepishly and looked at Enoch, dreading his scorn of my weak stomach.

His jaw was set and his face grim. Without a single word, he wet his bandanna from his canteen and wiped my trembling mouth with unsteady hands. I had to grit my teeth to keep from crying.

All the wagoners and walkers gathered horrified around the gruesome scene. Daniel caught my eye. He had an accusing expression, as if to say, "See!" I knew he was thinking this was all because of Quakers in the Assembly. I looked away.

There was Molly, white-faced, tears streaming down her cheeks. I recalled her asking, "Would ye be willin' to help me?"

I turned aside, shamed. What could I have done? My stomach heaved with another wave of nausea, but this time I managed to keep from vomiting.

The silence of the destroyed plantation, the mutilated bodies, pressed on all of us. We hated Indians more than ever. Instinctively we gathered around Jedediah.

He spoke in hushed tones, "This happened a day or so ago, but it still isn't safe even to bury these folks. We'll press on and report this outrage at Fort Cumberland. We should be there before nightfall. Keep your wagons as close together as you can and have your guns ready."

When we climbed back onto the buckboard, Enoch handed me the reins. I gripped them so hard that my knuckles went white. Enoch clutched his gun, ready to fire.

"What if you have to shoot someone?" I worried.

"What if we're shot at?" Enoch replied. "I'd shoot first and worry later."

"But the Meeting . . . "

"The Meeting isn't here. Nobody in Meeting has seen what we've just seen."

I said no more, but my thoughts raced on. What if we came home to find Pa and Will and Ben scalped,

Ma and Sheba hacked to pieces? My stomach lurched again.

All my life I'd been taught that there is that of God in everyone, even the worst of people. How could there be that of God in whoever had killed that family? I'd been taught that if strangers came, we should welcome them, offer them food, even a bed to sleep in. Had the murdered family done that? Were they Friends? Somehow, thinking of them as believers like us made the tragedy even worse.

If savages attacked us, would Friends' beliefs hold, or would Pa react like Enoch? The idea that Pa might not defend the family was terrifying, but if Pa threw aside peaceful ways, somehow that seemed even worse. The earth would shift!

What would *I* do? Could I look down a gun barrel at another human being and pull the trigger? How else could I protect Ma and Sheba from . . . what we had just seen? I struggled to find the answer, but I couldn't be certain. All I knew for sure was that Indians were evil, and that I was scared to death of them.

CHAPTER 9
Fort Cumberland

We were still tense as a fiddle string when the wagon train forded Wills's Creek where it flowed into the Potomac. Looking up, I saw natural terraces at least forty feet high. On the crest, the fort's palisade looked like an arrowhead pointed at the river. Behind the fort towered a forested mountain. I was sure glad we didn't have to cross that mountain!

As we strained up the far slope, we saw acres of clearing all the way to the fort. Pointed tree stumps stuck out of the barren ground like growing teeth. I was surprised. "Why would they cut down all the trees?" I wondered aloud.

Enoch snorted. "See that stockade? Where does thee think they got the logs to build it? Besides, clearing the land keeps the enemy from sneaking up on them."

Tents had occupied the cleared area, but where were the soldiers now? There was an abandoned feel about Fort Cumberland. Had the French and their savages attacked the fort?

Jedediah pulled his horn from his shirt and blew a couple of blasts. A lookout in one of the bastions yelled something, and a cheer rang out from inside the fort. We urged the horses on.

The palisade was made of newly hewn logs nine or

ten inches thick, close together, their points sticking up. I could barely see the roofs of long, low buildings behind them. The road followed the palisade for about a hundred feet. Then it jagged out in another bastion. A limp British flag hung from a pole.

Again Jedediah sounded his horn, and the main gate of the fort swung open. We drovers stayed with our wagons while Jedediah walked his horse through the gate. People inside came running out and surrounded us.

The men wore mostly civilian clothes, and even those were pretty ragged, a military cap here and there, or a tattered insignia. They looked sick. Some were wounded, hobbling around on crutches, their arms in dirty slings. Some looked too old to fight, or too young.

Women and children crowded around the sutler's wagon, chattering like a flock of starlings, eager to buy supplies. This wasn't at all what I expected a fort to be like.

An officer came out to meet Jedediah. "Sir, you are most welcome. I am Colonel Innes, the commanding officer. We've sent so many supplies with General Braddock that we are short of everything here. Whatever you have brought will be a great help."

"Has the general already marched? We hoped to supply his attack on Fort Duquesne." Jedediah was dismayed.

"Yes, sir, he has. The first troops left on May 29, and General Braddock and the most able-bodied soldiers set out shortly after. Those left here were physically unfit to make the trip. We are defending the fort until the general returns triumphant from the West."

"The very day we left Philadelphia! We were too late before we even set out!"

All of us groaned in chorus when we heard that news.

"But you are not too late for us," Colonel Innes assured him. "I've had to send details of men out every day to strip leaves from the forest for our horses. There's no grass or any other forage for miles around."

"Has General Braddock taken Fort Duquesne?" Jedediah asked.

"The army is still about two weeks east of there," Colonel Innes replied. "The expedition has been far more difficult than he anticipated. Woodcutters are hacking a road just in advance of the troops, wide enough for two wagons abreast and soldiers marching in formation."

"Yes, we've just been on your road from Virginia. We understand what you mean."

"The Alleghenies are more formidable than anyone anticipated," Colonel Innes continued. "Besides wagon-loads of supplies, our men are using block and tackle to lug cannons over these mountains."

"What about Indians?" Christopher asked.

"Small bands of Delaware and Shawanese have been attacking all along the way. Every day one or two soldiers are killed, not enough to stop the general's progress, but enough to frighten the men," Colonel Innes answered.

Jedediah pressed him. "Will any of our delivery be sent to the front?"

"Aye, sir, we'll forward some of the packhorses. Ours have been weakening and dying every day. The general will be as happy for replacements as for the feed they carry. Now, let's get your wagons unloaded and find space for your people to rest."

Colonel Innes issued swift orders, and men who looked as if they could scarcely move jumped to action. Quickly they unloaded all the wagons into two storehouses near the main gate.

Enoch and I watched our wagon being offloaded. Then an old soldier showed us where all the wagons would be left. When we had tended our horses, he led us back inside the fort.

Behind the headquarters cabin was a gap in the stockade. "Here's our parade ground," our guide said. "As ye c'n see, it's bigger than the front part. Beyond, ye'll find three cabins for officers. Behind each one o' them are two long barracks where us enlisted men sleep."

Each barrack had a door and one high window. There was no chinking between the logs. A stone fireplace faced the doorway. There were three sets of triple bunk beds on each side and pegs for coats. The barracks were no more than sleeping pens, but those were real beds.

"Here's where ye'll sleep t'night," the old man told us. "Since the troops left for Fort Duquesne, there's plenty of room for ye."

"What about supper?" Enoch asked.

"Generally, every soldier cooks his own rations at the fireplace here. But tonight, since ye've brought food, the women'll feed all of us a proper meal. It's been a long while since we've had more than spoiled meat to eat. At home, we could go out and gather berries in the woods and pull greens. But 't ain't safe to leave the fort, shorthanded as we are. Whatever ye've brought us, it'll seem a feast to the likes of us!"

That evening, the soldiers set up long trestle tables on the parade ground, and women did serve a "proper meal." We ate fresh meat and bread, stewed dried apples, Indian corn pudding, early carrots, and juicy cabbage. This was the best meal we had had since York. Colonel Innes served everyone a generous ration of rum to add to the festivities.

Later, I was startled to find Molly at my elbow.

"Has Charley gone with the general?" I asked.

"Aye, he must have. He's nowhere around here, at any rate. I'm sure the general would have taken Charley. He's strong and stout, not like these poor excuses for soldiers here."

"What will thee do?"

"I'll wait for him. He'll be back when they've taken Fort Duquesne. I've come too far to give up now! "

"Thee will wait here?"

"Aye, I'll find work to do and friends enough."

I was relieved. She always made me feel confused and clumsy. But I knew I would miss her on the trip home.

That night we could hear sentries calling out to each other as they patrolled. I felt safe inside the stockade. I was glad, too, for the comfort of a bed after so many nights on the ground.

But sleep wouldn't come. I couldn't stop thinking about those murdered settlers. Indians killed them, but the French put them up to it. So the French were as bad as the Indians, maybe even worse. And even if people *had* taken advantage of Indians, did that justify murder?

I turned on my side, my hands over my eyes. I could hear others tossing restlessly, so I wasn't the only one tortured by what we had seen. But nobody wanted to talk about it. I just wanted to put the day's nightmare behind me. Finally I did fall asleep, but then the night's bad dreams took over, a jumble of savages, screams, spurts of blood, and Enoch wiping my face.

The next morning soldiers rode out from the fort to find that plantation and scour the countryside for Indians and Frenchmen. I imagined myself with soldiers burying the victims and tracking down and finishing off their murderers. After that, I pictured the scene with soldiers defending the settlers. I saw my own gun blazing, enemies falling, settlers cheering. I tried both versions, but I still didn't know how I would act. Did I still believe there is that of God in everyone? Indians? The French? Even if I did, would I "turn the other cheek" and not resist?

The soldiers came back at dusk. They had seen neither Frenchmen nor Indians.

That evening Peter came in wearing a military cap. He looked both grim and excited. "I've joined up for three months," he announced. "There's no wagon or team to take back to Pa, so I might as well. Maybe I can help stop these attacks on settlers."

Most of the wagoners cheered, pounded his back, and praised his courage.

"Good for you, boy!"

"This outfit can surely use a stout lad like you!"

"It'll make a man of ye!"

Enoch and I said nothing. Then I suggested to him, "Let's go check on the horses." I wanted to talk with him in private.

After so many black nights in forests, the open sky above the fort felt good. Clusters of stars glittered overhead, and the cloudy Milky Way stretched farther than I could see.

A sentry swung his musket our way and called out, "Who goes there?"

"The Butlers, going to tend our horses," Enoch replied.

"The horses are fine. They're well guarded. But the gate is closed for the night. No one goes out or in but sentries. If you just want a smoke, go onto the parade ground."

So, swatting mosquitoes, we went to the parade ground. Enoch lit a pipe, to keep the skeeters at bay. The silence felt awkward. I wasn't sure how to talk with him about deep matters. He dealt only with facts. I sighed, wishing for Ben.

"Peter has joined the army," I stated finally.

"Aye."

"Does thee think he fears his pa that much?"

"Mayhap. Or mayhap the massacre raised his gorge."

"He didn't mention revenge. He said something about stopping attacks on settlers. Those are two different things, aren't they?"

Enoch stirred uneasily.

I pressed on. "Revenge means getting even, wanting to kill Indians because they killed settlers. Stopping attacks means preventing future massacres, isn't that right?"

"I suppose."

"We've been taught 'Vengeance is mine, saith the Lord.'" Doesn't that mean we should leave retribution to God, and not punish those that do harm?

"Aye, but Peter is not a Friend," Enoch reminded me.

"But do Friends have an obligation to stop attacks? Isn't that the responsible thing?"

"Is thee thinking of joining the army, too?" Enoch asked, half mockingly.

"I'm just trying to sort things out. A man must think on these matters."

"For me, the responsible thing is return the team and wagon, loaded with whatever of value we can find out here, and get home to Deborah. My wife is with child, my crops are planted, and I know where my responsibility lies."

"Aye, and Peter seems to know his."

Enoch's pipe had gone out, and he was tired of abstract thought. "'Tis time we returned to the barracks. The sentry will be wondering about us."

CHAPTER 10

Rescues in the Forest

Two days later, Jedediah summoned us into our usual line for the return trip. We felt refreshed after our rest in the fort, ready to set out again. We could feel the tug of duties at home. It was time for haying and nearly time to pull flax. There was always Indian corn to hoe. And all of us were eager to collect our twelve pounds in Philadelphia.

The wagon train was considerably smaller this time. Colonel Innes had persuaded a blacksmith and one of the wheelwrights to stay at Wills's Creek. Several women and children who had walked all the way from Philadelphia remained at Fort Cumberland to wait for their soldiers. Those who had come with their men could ride home in the emptied wagons, so no walkers were tagging along behind.

Many of our packhorses had already set out for General Braddock's western push. The rest carried enough feed for the teams to reach the Susquehanna, and from there on, grazing would be plentiful. Empty wagons travel farther in a day; our return would be swifter.

Peter sounded brave and sure of himself as he said goodbye to us. "Mayhap we'll meet again, Noble," he said. "Armies move around a lot. My enlistment is only three months, though, and then I'll be back on the farm."

"I wish thee well, Peter." I was sorry he was not going back with us, but I could think of nothing more to say.

As I climbed aboard the wagon, Molly pulled on my shirttail. "Goodbye, me friend," she murmured.

"Goodbye, Molly. I hope thy Charley comes safely back to thee."

Tears trembled on her lashes, but she jutted her chin out with determination. "And if he doesn't, then I will find me own way . . ."

Mayhap I hadn't seen the last of Molly.

Whips cracked, wagons creaked, and the train lumbered out through the heavy front gate of the fort. As it closed behind us, I realized how safe I had felt inside the fort. Now we were exposed to danger once more.

Scouts reported Indians were mostly to the west and south of Fort Cumberland. Colonel Innes had convinced Jedediah that we would be safer going north than returning the way we had come. So we followed Wills's Creek up the Cumberland Valley to Raystown.

Our narrow trail crossed the winding creek several times. The conestoga wagons broke branches on either side and widened the path as they pushed their way uphill. Enoch and I appreciated their going ahead of us.

Everyone stayed on full alert while Christopher and the other scouts patrolled. But apparently Colonel Innes' information had been correct. We saw no Indians all day.

Next morning Jedediah stopped the wagons at the top of a rise where trails intersected.

"Look, cleared fields!" exclaimed Horst.

"But no fences," Daniel pointed out. "No crops have been planted here for years."

A cluster of stone chimneys stood in the large clearing. Wild grapevines and woodbine wrapped around them. Tangled weeds poked up through charred timbers that had once supported roofs. What a sorry sight! Even one burned-out cabin speaks of calamity, and here were several within view of each other.

"How many died here?" I asked. "It looks like a whole community was destroyed."

"It didn't happen recently," Enoch said.

"Several tribes gather here every year for trade and ceremonies," Jedediah said. "They didn't mind white traders coming to do business. But when Scotch-Irish squatters settled here a few years ago, the tribes complained to the Assembly in Philadelphia."

"What did the Assembly say?" Daniel asked, sneering as if he already knew the answer.

"They asked the Scotch-Irish to leave because the settlers were violating treaties. But settlers dug in their heels and refused to budge."

"Sure they did. What happened next?" Daniel asked.

"The tribes appealed again. Their chief convinced the Assembly that he couldn't control his people if the Scotch-Irish stayed. So the Assembly sent a few Indian agents out here to dislodge the settlers. They still refused to leave, so the agents burned their cabins."

"Was anyone killed?" I asked, remembering what we had seen a few days ago.

"No. The Scotch-Irish were mad as hornets, of course, but they moved on. Most of them settled further down on the Juniata River."

"I guess that didn't satisfy the redskins," Daniel speculated. "They are on the warpath now."

Horst said, "Scotch-Irish won't listen to anyone! More push west every year. And the French! *Mein Gott in Himmel!* They make trouble here just like in the Old Country." He shook his head in exasperation.

Jedediah agreed. "Yes, when William Penn invited any and all to settle here, he opened the door to trouble."

I couldn't quit looking at the desolation. "Just think how hard these people worked." I said to Enoch. "Can thee imagine being forced off our farm?"

Enoch shook his head.

That afternoon, a piece of our rig broke. Enoch reined in the horses and jumped down.

"Need a hand?" Jedediah called as he rode past us.

"No, thanks. We can mend it."

"Well, hurry. Not seeing Indians doesn't mean we're safe."

Enoch waved him on. Several wagoners offered to help as they passed, but Enoch was sure he could repair it himself. He assured even the last drover, "We're nearly done."

Finally he finished, with a quick tug to test the correction. As he clucked to start the horses again, we realized we were alone on the road. The wagon train was out of sight.

Were Indians lurking behind the piles of cut trees lining this new road? I urged, "Faster, Enoch, faster! Catch up with the wagon train!"

"I'm going as fast as I can," Enoch said, whipping the reins. "With an empty wagon, we'd overturn if we went any faster."

As we rounded a bend, we heard something crashing through the forest on our left. A wild-looking man staggered out and collapsed onto the road right in front of us. The horses reared. Enoch fought to control them, and I grabbed the musket.

The man lay still, face down, in the middle of the road.

"Is he dead?"

"Looks like Indians got him!"

I jumped down to check him out.

"Be careful, Noble," Enoch warned.

"Look at that gash in his shoulder! Give me thy canteen."

Enoch swung the canteen down as I turned the man over. He peered up at me through glazed eyes. I raised the canteen to his lips, and he gulped the water down.

Finally he croaked, "Thank ye kindly."

"What is thy name, friend? What happened?" I asked.

"John McCowen. A redskin got me. Hit me with his tomahawk. Lost me balance. Fell backwards over the ridge."

"Thee needs more help than we can give," I said. "We'll be at McDowell's Mill by nightfall. Come with us."

"Nay!" John refused fiercely, lurching to his feet. "I'll not leave me pelts."

"Thy what?"

"Me pelts! I've been trappin' and tannin' in this gap all winter and spring, pinned down by Indian attacks. It's near six months' hard work. I canna leave them."

I glanced at Enoch, and he nodded. "Our wagon is empty," I said. "We can take thee and thy pelts. But hurry. We're already out of sight of the rest of the wagons."

John McCowen still hesitated. Then his knees buckled. "All right, then," he growled reluctantly. "They're stashed in a cave halfway up the mountain, well back inside. I canna get there meself, me head's a swimmin' so, but mayhap ye can make it."

I looked into the dark forest stretching up out of sight, and my heart sank. "Enoch," I said quickly, "I'll take care of John while thee gets the pelts."

"Nay," Enoch replied. "I'm minding the team and wagon. But be quick!"

So I gritted my teeth and plunged into the thick forest. No path, and briars everywhere. I grabbed sapling after sapling between the giant trees to pull myself up, using roots as stairs. Where was John's cave?

I hauled myself around a large maple and rested a minute against its broad trunk. This didn't seem a likely place for a cave. I began to wonder whether John's cave was only his feverish imagination.

Why was I risking life and limb for someone I didn't even know? Was it worth all this effort? I heard the horses on the road below, stamping nervously. I drew a deep breath and pressed on. Above was a ledge extending to the right. If I could make it to that ledge, I might find the opening to the cave.

Placing my feet carefully and holding onto branches and roots, I finally reached a narrow shelf between the edge of the cliff and a sheer rock wall. I could make out a faint path, so this must be the right place. Overhead, I saw gnarled roots and spreading branches of a beech tree hanging out over the ledge. I could almost hear Pa saying, "Don't play under a beech, Noble. Those trees can drop a limb at any time, without even a breeze to stir them."

A needless caution, like so many of Pa's wise sayings. How many times had I played under a beech, even gathered nuts, and I'd never seen a branch let go.

I brushed against a curtain of vines that just might hide the mouth of a cave. Cautiously I lifted the outer edge. Yes! This must be it! I pushed through the vines into a black hole.

A suffocating darkness swallowed all the light. Clammy, cave-cold air wrapped around me. I stood stark still, waiting for my eyes to adjust, listening intently. I heard nothing. Then my nose tingled at the smells of leather and ashes.

Relieved, I flailed backwards, sweeping open the blind of brambles. Long fingers of afternoon sun quivered into the low cave and pointed to stacks of stiff, dried hides bound with rawhide straps. Bales of pelts stacked beside them proved John's claim of a winter's work. Curing frames lined the walls, and cold ashes filled a fire pit well back in the cavernous room. The skins were worth a fortune. But how could I get them to the wagon? Should I just tumble them down the way John landed?

From the cave, I could barely see the road below. Enoch was looking impatiently up the hill. The horses shook their heads and tossed the reins.

One after the other, I flung the bales down the cliff. I completely forgot about Indians. I grunted as I heaved each load over the ledge. I groaned as a bundle lodged in. I whooped in triumph as the last bale went over the edge.

Then I scrabbled together a few traps and snare ropes and threw them after the pelts. The traps banged against rocks and trees. Some of the ropes tangled and snagged along the way.

I heard the screech of tearing timber. I looked up and saw a branch shearing off the beech on the cliff above. The limb, nearly tree-size itself, scraped down the embankment and landed just a few feet from where I stood, blocking the path.

My heart pounded. I could almost hear Pa saying, "I warned thee, Noble!"

Then I gasped in terror. I was looking directly into the hostile eyes of an Indian behind that fallen branch! He was nearly invisible in the mottled sunlight. His face was somehow marked so he looked like a wolf. The end of his nose was black, and his eyes were outlined in black to look like an animal's eyes. Black lines ran from the point of his chin up along his jaws clear to the tops of his ears. A terrible grimace contorted his face. He stood erect, perfectly motionless.

My mind reeled.

How did he slip up on me unnoticed?

How many more savages were hiding, ready to attack?

Was this the one who attacked John McCowen?

Visions of massacred settlers filled my mind. Was this their murderer? Was I next?

I opened my mouth to shout a warning to Enoch, but no sound, not even a squeak, came out. I fully expected a tomahawk to come hurtling in my direction, and I was too scared even to duck. I felt nailed to the spot where I would surely die.

The Indian and I stared at each other silently for what seemed like forever.

Nothing happened. Nothing!

I looked more closely. He seemed about my age, maybe even younger, and he might be a Delaware, I thought. His teeth were clenched, and the muscles in his face worked in spasms.

Then I realized he was in pain. And no wonder! That fallen limb was bearing on his left foot, and he was pinned to the cliff. If he tried to work his way out, the whole thing would pull him over the edge. There was no way he could free himself.

I drew a deep breath and my muscles unlocked. My first instinct was to offer to help, but I hesitated. I needed to get out of there as fast as I could.

But this person was suffering! Shouldn't I help him somehow? Isn't that what I had been taught? All the years of Quaker training rose within me.

If I helped, he could kill me. If I called for Enoch, that might alert the rest of his tribe.

But he was trapped and suffering. Would he die if I didn't help him? Wouldn't that be the same as killing him?

But if I freed him, wouldn't he endanger the entire wagon train?

On the other hand, he was wounded and needed help. Wasn't that why we were helping John McCowen?

I looked again at the Indian's set expression. If I ignored his need and made my way back to the wagon.... No, I just couldn't turn away.

I wished we spoke the same language!

Then I seemed to hear Ma's voice: *Look for that of God within him, and he will respond to that of God within thee.*

I took a deep breath and stretched out both hands to this lad, palms up, and said as softly as I could, "I see thee is trapped. May I help thee?"

He tensed even more but said nothing. I moved slowly toward him, speaking gently. "I mean thee no harm. I will move the branch, and we can each go our own way."

Still there was no answer, no change of expression.

As I got closer, his hand moved toward his knife, his eyes full of hatred.

I tried to ignore my quivering knees and center my thoughts, focus on holding him in the Light. I worked my way carefully behind the branch, hoping it would not topple both of us over the edge. At last I stood beside him. Our backs were pressed against the cliff wall. Then, slowly, I disentangled enough branches that he could help lift with one hand. Together we shoved the fallen limb over the edge. Both of us breathed sighs of relief.

I whistled softly. A bone was sticking out of his shoulder, white against his dark flesh. The jagged trunk had crushed one foot. Bloody scratches from the branches covered him.

"Is there more I can do to help thee?" I asked, regretting again the language barrier.

He only made a brusque motion for me to be on my way.

But I hesitated, looking around. I found a forked stick, fashioned it into a rude crutch and offered it to him. He accepted it with a curt nod and again waved me away.

My heart pounding, I slid down the hill, dislodging ropes and pelts along the way. Finally I tumbled onto the road almost as John had. There beside Enoch and John was the scout Christopher, trying to control his horse, which was circling impatiently. Both Christopher and Enoch held guns at ready and were scanning the forest for signs of danger. John, barely conscious, was propped against the rear wheel. The wagon was loaded.

"What took thee so long?" Enoch complained.

"Were there signs of Indians up there? Christopher asked.

I cut off their questions. "Let's get John into the wagon and catch up with the rest of the train."

The three of us hoisted John atop the piles of fur. Enoch and I jumped onto the buckboard. Enoch flicked the horses' rumps with his whip to get them going. Christopher galloped ahead. Our rickety wagon gathered speed, going more smoothly now that it was loaded.

The declining sun felt good on my sweat-drenched back, and the breeze cooled my face. The horses' pounding gallop kept pace with my racing thoughts.

What had I just done? Had I released a heathen murderer who would kill again?

He was wounded enough that he couldn't kill for a while, but what about the rest of his tribe? Would they attack the wagon train? And wouldn't it be my fault if they did?

But he was just a lad, mayhap younger than I. His pain was real, and he might have died if I hadn't freed him.

Daniel would say I should have killed him, given the chance.

But he was a real person, someone I had met, sort of. We had looked each other in the eye, worked together to dislodge that branch, communicated somehow. Like John McCowen, he needed help. I couldn't kill him.

But if he told his tribe and they attacked the wagon train, wouldn't it be my fault?

I needed to tell someone about what had just happened. I glanced at Enoch urging the horses faster and faster. He would either think it a tall tale or berate me for a fool. Christopher was out of sight around the next bend, and who knew how far ahead the rest of the wagon train might be by now.

Filled with dread, I resolved to tell Jedediah or Christopher at the first opportunity.

CHAPTER 11

McDowell's Mill

Our wagon rumbled up to McDowell's Mill at sunset. Conococheague Creek cascaded over the falls where the huge, three-story mill stood. Its overshot waterwheel waited silently.

That mill was the largest building I had seen since we left the wharves of Philadelphia. In fact, here in the wilderness, it looked even bigger than the warehouses at the port. Its stone foundation seemed part of the creek bank. The black walls were made of solid upright beams.

I had often taken loads of grain to our local mill in Chester County, but McDowell's Mill was different. Surrounding the mill and the McDowells' cabin was the beginning of a stockade.

Mr. McDowell was anxious to let us in to the mill, where all of us wagoners were to sleep. Jedediah was relieved to see us.

"I was sure the Delaware had got you. I couldn't risk the rest of the train to find you, but I sent Christopher. What delayed you?"

"Fixing the harness took longer than I expected," Enoch explained, "and then we picked up a passenger. This is John McCowen. An Indian got him."

"Where? When? How close are they to the fort?"

"We didn't see any. We found John in the gap, but I think the attack happened a couple of days ago," Enoch said. "Can anyone here tend his wound?"

"Bring him on in. Mrs. McDowell will have a look at him."

Mrs. McDowell bustled up, her cap askew, her stays loosened for comfort. "Who do we have here? Why, Johnnie McCowen, is it? Ach, laddie, what happened to ye?" She turned to Enoch and me. "Carry 'im into the house, and I'll have a look at 'im."

Not waiting for a reply, she led us into her cabin next to the mill. This was not the time to talk to Jedediah or Christopher. Too much commotion, too many people around.

Enoch left as Mrs. McDowell seated John on a bench and began to tend his wounded shoulder, but I stuck around. Shreds of his grimy shirt were embedded in his flesh where the tomahawk had struck. Bits of dried leaves and twigs were ground in as well.

Mrs. McDowell clucked to herself as she washed the gash. When John stiffened and exclaimed with pain, she gave him a dram of rum. Then she returned to her work, sponging away dirt and caked blood. She mixed a poultice of herbs and honey in a small linen bag and pressed it to the wound. Then she wrapped his shoulder round and round with strips of linen.

"There, laddie, that's the best I can do fer ye. Now tell me, what are ye doin' still in these parts? Yer family left weeks ago!"

"They left? Why? Where have they gone?"

"Aye, they left, like the sensible folk they are, them and most of the other settlers. Because of the savages, laddie. How come ye not to know these things? Have ye been asleep in the woods like a hibernatin' bear?"

"Yes, ma'am, I guess ye could call it that. I've been trappin' in the mountains since early spring, and I couldna' get out for the redskins pesterin' me. So I was trapped meself. But me family's gone? Gone where? When?"

"Let me think. I believe they said Easton. Yes, Easton. Have ye kin in Easton? They left weeks ago, takin' all they could pile inta their wagon, leadin' the cow and calf along behind. I thought you was with 'em, but there's so many of ye McCowen laddies that I didn't bother to count. Did they know where ye was trappin'?"

"Not exactly, no, ma'am. What did you mean, because of the savages?"

"Why, Johnnie, the frontier's gone daft! Indians attackin' men in the fields, walkin' right in on a family at table, butcherin' and stealin' all the white folk in the valley. People are that frightened that they leave new-seeded fields and flee for safety to the east. Yer family must have thought the heathen had already got ye. They had no way to reach ye, so they could only pray the best for ye and save themselves. Tsk, tsk, tsk!"

I gulped, thinking of the Delaware I had rescued.

John McCowen struggled to remain conscious, fighting waves of pain. But he managed to ask, "Then why are ye still here, ye and yer man McDowell?"

"Because the mill is here, and we've no livelihood without the mill. We can't pack it up and take it with us, so we're tryin' to build a stockade around it. In fact, when yer wagon train arrived, the men all pitched in and cut trees and set them deep in the ground. A good thing, too. There are still a few families left here in Shearman's

Valley, and they need us to mill their grain. If an attack comes, the neighbors'll all take refuge here in the mill."

Then she remembered I was there, too. "Here I am a-chatterin' away and the twa of ye hungry! Let me give ye both some supper. The rest hae already eaten, but there's some porridge and milk left. After all this time in the woods, ye could do wi' some cooked food, nae doubt!"

She ladled porridge into wooden bowls and dipped milk from a tin bucket over the steaming gruel. She gave each of us a spoon and watched us eat. I gobbled mine down, but John could hardly swallow. He looked ashen from pain.

When we finished, she said, "Now, Johnnie, the men frae yer wagon train are sleepin' in the mill tonight, but I think I'll keep ye here wi' McDowell and me, to keep an eye on ye. Yer young friend can collect ye in the mornin' when the train leaves."

I was startled. "Shouldn't John stay here to get well?"

"Oh, it's nae possible! He won't mend here a-tall! He needs much care, and I hae no skill nor medicines. Even if I did, we need to spend every minute buildin' our stockade. This is no place for an invalid! Besides, he needs ta find his family."

"But Easton is a long way off," I protested. "We're not going that far."

Mrs. McDowell looked at me intently. "Well, laddie, in times like these, we do what we must. Not only would he weaken and die here, but he would be in the way. Ye brought Johnnie here, and I've done me best for him. Now ye must take him with ye. Or," she said brutally, "ye could leave him to die in the woods, I suppose. But whatever ye decide, he canna stay here."

I was aghast. How could she reject someone she knew? My family would care for John as one of us, no matter the risk. We would trust God and do whatever needed to be done.

But I could see her logic. John wasn't the only one in danger. She was thinking of her family and the neighbors. Tending a wounded man would take time. She needed to run the mill while her husband and the neighbors built the stockade. John, whose own family had left without him, would put everyone else at risk.

John had sunk onto the pallet Mrs. McDowell had spread for him near the hearth. His eyes were closed and his face expressionless. I wondered whether he had heard this conversation.

"Sleep well, John," I muttered. "I'll see thee in the morning." I went back to the mill, more exhausted than I had ever been.

Horst, on sentry duty, opened the creaking door. The mill had the homey smell of grain. I scanned the dimly lit floor, lumpy with bags of flour and snoring wagoners, to find Enoch.

But tired as I was, there was one more thing I must do before I could sleep. I must tell someone about the Delaware I had freed. I spotted Christopher and Jedediah deep in conversation on the second floor.

Stepping around the wagoners, I trudged up the broad stairsteps. Christopher motioned for me to sit on a bag of wheat. I plopped down and wiped some of the sweat off my face.

"What happened when you were getting McCowen's pelts, Noble? I heard a crash that had nothing to do with pelts, then another a few minutes before you tumbled onto the road. I could tell by the way you avoided your brother's eyes you were hiding something."

I looked from Christopher to Jedediah and back to Christopher. Sighing, I said, "The first crash was a huge limb falling from a beech tree."

"They don't call beech trees 'widow makers' for nothing," Jedediah said.

"I had just emptied the cave and was ready to come back to the wagon when it fell. I looked around, and there was an Indian pinned between the branch and the wall of the cliff. I was pretty scared. I didn't know what to do. I couldn't just leave him there, so I helped him get free. The second crash was the branch falling off the cliff."

"You freed him?" Jedediah exclaimed. "What were you thinking? He could have killed you on the spot! Even worse, now he'll live to ambush the wagon train and attack settlers! You freed a redskin!" he repeated in disbelief.

"I thought about all that, but he was wounded. A bone was sticking out of his shoulder, and the limb had landed on his foot. I couldn't just leave him there suffering."

"What did he do then?" Christopher asked.

"He waved me away. But I made him a sort of crutch first. He took it and motioned me away again. Then I slid down the hill as fast as I could and landed on the road."

"You even made him a crutch!" Jedediah' scorn was withering. "Did you tell him we were spending this night at the mill?"

I hung my head. "Of course not," I mumbled.

"What did he look like?" Christopher asked.

"He's about my age and size. His face was marked so he looked like a wolf.

"That was Broken Blade," Christopher said. "Did he have his knife with him?"

"Yes. He couldn't get to it while he was pinned by the branch, but afterwards, he didn't try to use it. He just waved me off."

"No, he wouldn't use it at that point. The fact that you saved his life is what saved yours. Broken Blade is very proud. Now that he owes his life to you, he wouldn't harm you in any way."

Jedediah interrupted, "But that doesn't mean he wouldn't attack the wagon train, does it?"

"No. That wouldn't change his attitude toward all the rest of us. If he attacked our train and recognized Noble, he'd spare him and kill everyone else."

I felt cold inside.

"How do you know this heathen?" Jedediah asked Christopher. "What do you know about him?"

"He's a Lenapé, the tribe you call Delaware. After the Walking Purchase, his family ended up in the Wyoming Valley. Then squatters forced them out of there."

"But how do you know him?" Jedediah persisted.

"I spent last winter in his village. His craw is full of bitterness against Coat Men. That's what he calls white people. He came after me one day with his knife. I pulled mine, and we went at it for a bloody while. Then I dodged when he threw his knife at me. It landed on a rock, and the blade broke. His name was already Broken Blade, and when the knife broke, he sorta broke, himself.

All the fight went out of him." Christopher shook his head at the memory.

He went on, "He wanted to kill me, but the chief told him it was tribal hospitality to take me in. I would have frozen solid in the woods trying to make it back home that late in the season. The chief said if Broken Blade caused any more trouble, he would be cast out of the village himself. The chief and I had done business together, so he trusted me. Gradually Broken Blade began to get used to me. Finally he told me his story. He has reason to be bitter. You were lucky that tree limb pinned him, Noble. He was likely near to killing you."

"Did you see any others?" Jedediah asked.

"No, nor hear any. I think he was alone."

"And why didn't you tell me right away?" Christopher asked.

"I wanted out of there fast. Enoch was already complaining. Then thee rode on ahead, and I was worried about John McCowen . . ."

"Who is this John McCowen?" Jedediah asked.

"He was attacked by a redskin and left for dead. He'd been trapping for months and wouldn't leave his pelts. So we offered to bring him and his pelts this far."

"Does he have family around here?" Jedediah asked.

"They've left for Easton. Mrs. McDowell knows them, but she won't let John stay here at the mill. She says we have to take him with us tomorrow," I said.

"How bad is he hurt?" asked Christopher.

"There's an ugly gash in his shoulder. Mrs. McDowell cleaned it and put a poultice on it. But he's weak as a kitten. He couldn't eat the supper she gave us."

"Well, she's no nurse, and they have a stockade to build," Jedediah said. "I don't suppose John will slow us down. If he does, you may get left behind. Once we cross the Susquehanna again you should be safe enough. Are you and your brother willing to take him?"

"I came just now from McDowells' cabin, and Enoch is already asleep."

"In the morning, then, you two decide what to do with him. He needs to get to his family in Easton, but it may take a long time to heal that wound."

Christopher interrupted, "Get some rest, Noble. Let us know what you've decided."

Dog-tired, I stumbled back down the heavy planks of the staircase. I stepped over snoring wagoners and stretched out beside my brother near the back wall.

The talk with Jedediah and Christopher had gone pretty well, I thought. Pa reacted worse than they did whenever I broke a rule. But there were life or death consequences from what I had done.

I believed I really had saved Broken Blade's life. I was sure we had saved John McCowen's life, so far, but now we were responsible for him.

A part of Christopher's story echoed in my mind: "*The chief told him it was a matter of tribal hospitality to take me in because I would die if I tried to make it back to my home.*"

Indians would shelter an enemy to save his life, but Mrs. McDowell wouldn't shelter even someone she knew. Quakers would. My family would, for sure.

I fell into a troubled sleep, the words *responsibility* and *hospitality* tumbling in my dreams along with scenes of Indian villages, gristmills, and our farm.

CHAPTER 12
The Way Home

In the gray time between night and morning, I woke up before anyone else. My head was buzzing with a plan. At Enoch's first stir, I whispered, "I have to talk to thee."

He sat up and rubbed his face. I reached a hand to pull him to his feet. Then we tiptoed to the door. The sentry grunted a sleepy greeting.

We climbed onto the buckboard and sat side by side. I waited through another few minutes of Enoch's yawning and stretching, and then he said, "What does thee want this early?"

"Last night Mrs. McDowell said they can't keep John. She said we could either take him with us or leave him to die in the woods."

Enoch stared blankly. "What in the world will *we* do with him?"

"Remember Pa said not to come home with an empty wagon? Ma could nurse John back to health, and we could sell his pelts for him in Philadelphia."

Enoch slowly took in what I was proposing. Then he said, "Traders pay trappers maybe half the price pelts bring in Philadelphia."

I nodded. "Let's offer John seventy-five percent. Those are fine pelts, and there are lots of them. It would be a good business deal for him and for us."

Enoch asked, "How long will it will take him to recover?"

"I don't know."

"Ma's a good nurse, and she's teaching Sheba. Between them, he should mend well."

I wanted to whoop with relief, but I just heaved a deep, contented sigh.

Enoch went on, "We need to ask Jedediah, since we'll be adding a member to the train."

"He told me last night it was up to us. We'll have to convince John, though."

The sky was brightening when we returned to the mill. Jedediah quickly agreed to our plan. Then we knocked on McDowells' door to speak to John.

Mrs. McDowell opened the door, nodded to us, and called over her shoulder to John, "On yer feet, laddie. Here's yer rescuers come to fetch ye."

John stumbled to his feet. He looked a little better than the night before. Mrs. McDowell gave each of us a mug of ale and a chunk of bread.

I cleared my throat and said, "John, Mrs. McDowell says thee must leave with us. So here's our plan. We'll take thee and thy pelts to our farm in Chester County. Ma will nurse thee back to health, and Enoch and I will sell thy pelts for thee in Philadelphia. What does thee say?"

"Quakers are too clever. You'd fleece me of my pelts," John growled.

"Thee can trust us," I assured him. "Because we are Friends, we are as good as our word. We'll look after thy health and get thee a fair price for thy pelts."

Enoch added, "We'll give thee seventy-five percent of whatever we can sell them for."

"That's generous!" John exclaimed. "But what will your family say when ye show up with an extra man, and him not able to work?"

"As I said, we are Friends, and hospitality is one of our practices. Besides, Ma is a fine nurse. Thee will be in good hands." I avoided looking at Mrs. McDowell.

"And why would ye do this for me, a stranger? Because of me pelts?"

"Nay," I replied. "We would help thee with or without them. We don't need to sell the pelts, but we could get a good price for them."

"When thee is strong again, thee can find thy family," Enoch added.

John hesitated.

"Yer not likely to get a better offer, laddie," Mrs. McDowell prompted. "Ye'd best swaller yer pride and gae with 'em. Ye've nothin' to lose and much to gain."

John shook his head in disbelief. "Well, thank ye kindly. I'll repay ye when I can." He thanked Mrs. McDowell and followed us out to the wagon, cradling his left arm in his right hand. Every step he took seemed to hurt his wounded shoulder.

I settled John on the pelts. Then I climbed onto the buckboard beside Enoch as the train pulled out of the Mill. From time to time I glanced over my shoulder to check on John.

Sometimes he dozed, but other times he seemed hungry for conversation after so many months alone in the mountains. Finally he said, "Noble, climb over the buckboard and come on back here. These pelts are softer than that plank ye're sittin' on."

I was glad for the invitation. Enoch couldn't be bothered with talk. I'd been lonely and hungry for someone to talk to, too. I scrambled over and sank onto the pile of furs.

"I've ne'er known Quakers," John said. "Now that I'll be stayin' wi' ye a while, I'm wonderin' what it'll be like. Is it just ye and Enoch, or do ye have a passle of brothers like I do?"

This was a good time to break the family rule about not talking about private matters. After all, John was going home with us. He might as well know what to expect. Trying not to worry about what Enoch would think, I plunged right in. "Enoch here is my oldest brother, and he's married to Deborah. Their baby will come in a few months. Next is our sister, Sheba, then William, then me, and last is Benjamin. All of us but Enoch live at home with Ma and Pa."

"Ah, ye have a sister!" John sighed. "In the McCowen clan we're all lads. I'm the first-born. We have a William, too. He's next to me, then Finlaw, Duncan, and Daniel. Ma's had a rough go with a cabin full of boys and no daughters to give her a hand."

I'd never considered before just how much Sheba helped Ma. What would Ma ever do without her when she married?

"And do ye live in Philadelphia?" John asked.

"Nay, we have a plantation in Chester County. It's half a day's drive into the city."

"A plantation!" John exclaimed. "That's over a hundred acres! That must be a lot of work. So what in the world are ye doin' out here in the back country? How can yer pa spare ye?"

"The crops are all planted, and it's too early for harvest.

There's little to do this month but haying, and the folks can manage that without me."

"Even so, what made ye want to leave comfort and safety to come way out here?"

So I filled John in on the news he'd missed holed up in his cave for all those months.

He mulled it all over for a while, and then he blurted out, "I thought ye were Quakers. Quakers don't believe in fightin', do they? So how can ye in clear conscience supply an army?"

"These soldiers have come to our aid. We see nothing wrong in supplying them with food. Besides, it's a chance to earn some money and to see the West."

"I'm fer earnin' money meself. That's why I've been trappin' in the mountains all these months. I'm hopin' to help me father get clear title to the farm. What do you need money for?"

Enoch had heard all he could stand. "That's enough, Noble. Let John rest."

I climbed back to the front of the wagon.

John dozed and roused and dozed again. He sat up whenever we overtook settlers fleeing eastward. They seemed to fill the road. He peered into their faces but didn't know any of them. I looked at that miserable stream of refugees and shook my head. Where would they go? We could take care of John, but who would house all these people? Did they have kinfolk back East?

I just couldn't imagine a family abandoning a son, even a grown-up one. The McCowens must have been scared to death.

Late afternoon, John got all feverish again. His groaning jostled me out of my thoughts. I offered him the canteen, and he drank a great draught. I wrapped my bedroll around him and put Enoch's under his head.

I remembered how tenderly Ma had nursed me the last time I had a fever. Her hand had been so cool on my brow, her voice so soothing. She had a corner of the kitchen garden for medicinal herbs and always knew just the right ones for every illness. If we could just get John home to Ma, he'd survive.

"Rest easy, John," I told him. "We're getting home as fast as we can."

"'Tis lucky ye are to have a home to go to! I guess my family is out in the cold again!"

"What does thee mean, John?"

"This is the third time we McCowens have been forced off our land. We thought for sure we'd be safe in Shearman's Valley, but here we go again!"

"Indians have attacked thee before?"

"Nay, not Indians. First time it was the British, forcin' crofters out durin' the Clearances in Scotland. I was but a wee laddie, but I remember the soldiers with muskets and dogs, chasin' us through the heather and gorse. I can still see the flames against the night sky as our cottage burned. We got away, me parents and all me brothers, and made our way across the sea. Then we went up the Susquehanna into the back country of Pennsylvania, along with others of our clan. There was all this empty land, well cleared, with only a few footpaths criss-crossin' it, ready to farm. So we built cabins, plowed fields, and settled in."

I glanced at Enoch. Was this where we had seen the burnt cabins two days ago? Enoch was listening, but he didn't turn around.

"'Twas a bonnie sight, all those cabins in a cluster, surrounded by fields in all directions. Then the redskins came and told us to leave. Said it was their gatherin' place. We were welcome to trade there, but not to settle. They claimed the land was theirs. Of course we weren't about to give up what we had worked on so hard. We told 'em we wouldn't bother their gatherin's, but we had crops in the ground and intended to stay. They left, and we thought that might be the end of it, but we kept our guns handy, just in case.

"Then a few months later a tough lookin' lot showed up from the Assembly in Philadelphia. Said they had orders to put us off the land. Me father and the others argued with 'em, but 'twas no use. They pulled guns, ordered all of us out of our houses, and set fire to 'em. Burned out again, same as in the Old Country. And now, five years of back-breakin' work later, me family has fled to Easton!"

John slumped back onto his soft bed. His face was flushed, from fever or anger. I couldn't think of a single comforting thing to say.

His story sounded a lot like what Christopher had told me about Broken Blade. Squatters had put Broken Blade's family off their land two different times, and now he wanted revenge against any white person, not just those that wronged him. So all this squabbling over land led to war, and even people who hadn't taken other people's property got sucked into fighting.

War changes people into . . . what? Into savages, seems like. I used to think if I could fight, war might make me a man. Well, I had seen no battles, but surely manhood must be more than destruction and revenge.

I shook my head in frustration with the whole stupid mess.

The next morning, Jedediah said we should get to Harris's Ferry on the west side of the Susquehanna by nightfall. Enoch ran the horses as fast as they could go all day.

John's fever had broken about dawn, and he was restless. "C'mon back here, Noble. Let's pass the time talkin' again. Are ye the youngest of the wagoners in this train?"

"I suppose I am now. On the way out, Peter and Molly were with us. But Peter's wagon went over the side of a mountain, so he joined the militia and stayed at Fort Cumberland. Molly stayed, too, to wait for her man Charley, a soldier with General Braddock's army."

"Peter joined the militia? I might do that meself when me shoulder mends. Now who is this Molly ye mentioned?"

I chewed on my lower lip and squirmed on the bearskin. I'd been trying not to think about Molly ever since she told me goodbye at the fort. She was exciting and scary at the same time. The only girls I knew were from the Meeting, and none of them ever acted like Molly. I had to wonder what might have happened if Enoch hadn't always butted in. My imagination could take me only so far.

Seeing my discomfort, John teased, "Ye did mention a Molly, did ye not?"

"She's a girl from Philadelphia who joined the wagon train to find her man Charley."

"Aye, ye told me that much already. Is there no story about Molly?"

My Quaker training kicked in. "There is, but it's not for me to tell. Molly just asked me to be her friend on the trail and help her if she needed aid."

"And did ye?"

"Nay, she was safe enough."

"And how were you her friend on the trail?"

True to form, Enoch interrupted. "Noble, let's swap places and I'll catch a nap."

In the afternoon, John's fever rose, so I gave him more water. His hands moved restlessly. He muttered about setting traps and stretching skins on frames, things he'd done during those long months in his cave.

That night on the dark bank of the Susquehanna, John cried out in delirium, thrashing around in the wagon bed. Finally, after the moon went down, he quieted. His fever had finally broken, but we were pretty sure it would rise again next day.

Before dawn, I heard Jedediah asking John Harris, "Is the river too high for us to ford? I'd hate to have to camp until the water gets back to a safe level."

"No, it's less than three feet deep. You can walk your wagons across today," Harris said.

Jedediah called Enoch and me aside. "Since John seems to be worsening, you should cross first. Mr. Harris says you'll be safe going on alone, so don't wait for the rest of us."

"Thanks," I replied. "The sooner we get him home to Ma, the better his chances."

So we said our goodbyes and led our team into the river.

This crossing was about twenty-five miles upstream

from Wright's Ferry as the crow flies. Here the river was only half as wide, and shallow. I could easily see the rocks worn smoother than most of the roads we had traveled.

As Enoch held the reins, I looked down into the rushing river. I thought of the course it must follow to Wright's Ferry, over rocks, around bends, sometimes shallow, sometimes deep. A floating branch looked like the one Broken Blade and I had shoved over the side of the cliff. The river swept everything along.

I myself felt swept away by the past few weeks. When I left home, I set out on a grand adventure. Instead, I found knotty questions and tragedies.

I had wondered how people lived out there. Now I had seen settlers, soldiers, tribes, all frustrated by each other's needs. I had never given a single thought to who might have owned our land before us or where they were now.

Whenever I had seen an Indian in Philadelphia, I always tried not to stare. Now I had seen one eyeball to eyeball and even rescued him. That Indian was a real person. A person in trouble. How could I not help him? Had I gone soft, then? I didn't think so, but Jedediah sure did. No Indians attacked the wagon train, but if they had, it would have been my fault.

I had thought I could be part of teaching Indians that they couldn't treat white people that way. Instead, I had spared one Indian who would now kill any white settler he saw except me. How would I feel as the only survivor? Guilty, for sure.

But hearing Broken Blade's story, I could see why the Delaware hate us. What kind of lesson could we teach them? They had already learned we are not to be trusted.

I still wanted to protect my family, but I knew less than ever how to do that. For me, war itself was beginning to feel like an enemy, and how could I ever stop a war?

The profit Enoch and I would share at journey's end now seemed petty. Tools I wanted could only turn wood into furniture. They couldn't set things right between whites and Indians.

Seeing the water swirl below the wagon, I felt a lot older than I was just a month ago.

After the crossing, we left the mountains behind. Forested uplands sloped eastward downhill. We began to see tidy German farms and then Quaker plantations. Their thick-walled stone houses looked solid and enduring compared to crude log cabins in the Back Counties. Fields and gardens were laid out in squares rather than helter-skelter around tree stumps. Everything seemed so . . . so orderly.

We passed Friends meeting houses with separate doors for men and women and long sheds for horses. They looked like our Goshen Meeting, where I sat in the back with other lads. We tormented each other silently during the long silences while the grown-ups waited for the Spirit to move them. I had been so bored by it all. But I must have absorbed the Quaker beliefs. I had tested some of them on this trip, and they seemed to stand, in spite of Daniel's scorn.

Enoch was as much concerned about John as I was. We had become partners. We were racing against time in homespun clothes on our old farm wagon, not in colorful uniforms or mounted on powerful steeds, but we were doing something good, not destructive. If only we could get home before John gave out on us. He grew weaker with every mile, and his wound smelled rotten.

CHAPTER 13

Home at Last

Two days later we turned into our own lane, just as Sheba blew the ram's horn to call Pa and Will and Ben in for supper. It reminded me of Jedediah's trumpet blasts when we got to Fort Cumberland, only this seemed so much sweeter. It echoed past the orchard and barns and reached out to draw us in. We could almost make out the smell of supper floating on that sound.

Enoch drove right up to the front door. Ma and Sheba came running out to welcome us.

"We've been looking for ye for days!" Sheba exclaimed.

"And here ye are, safe and sound," Ma's smile lit up her whole face.

Enoch only nodded with his wry half-grin. He hurried past them up the steps and into the parlor to make a bed for John.

Just then John let out one of his groans. Startled, Ma and Sheba stood on tiptoe to look over the side of the wagon. They saw a sandy-haired, flushed-faced stranger thrashing feverishly on a rumpled pile of fur pelts.

"Who is he?" Ma asked. "What has happened to him?"

"John McCowen," I answered. "He's been tomahawked, and his wound has turned putrid. We thought thee could nurse him back to health, if he isn't too far gone. We'll tell thee all about it later. Right now, let's get John into the house."

Enoch had pulled out a bed and was ready for us. He and I half-carried, half-dragged John up the front steps and into the parlor. We laid him down as gently as we could and covered him with a blanket. He was shivering, though his skin felt as if he was burning up. Sheba held a cup of cool water to his lips. His eyes were glittery with fever, but he gave her a weak smile.

Then Ma took over. "Look at those red streaks under his bandage! That's a bad sign." She tried to help him take off his shirt, but it was stuck in his wound. She brought a basin of warm water and a soft rag and sponged away at it until it came loose. Then she cut away the bandage and gently washed the wound. She always crooned soft, soothing sounds when she was nursing anyone. No matter how much it hurt, Ma made it seem like everything would be fine.

A rank stench of putrefaction, sweat, and pelts filled the parlor. Sheba made a face, pinched her nose, and turned to leave the room, but Ma called her back.

Pa and Will and Ben came in from the field where they had been haying all day. Pa clapped Enoch and me on the shoulder and said, "Glad to see thee. Looks like an interesting load in the wagon. Who's our guest?"

While Enoch explained, Ma pulled Ben aside. "Bring me a few leeches from the creek. This wound needs bleeding."

Ben could hardly stand to be sent away, but he did as he was told. He was back in no time with a bucket of the gray wigglers.

Ma applied them to the red streaks radiating from John's wound. The leeches clamped themselves on and began sucking. When they were fat with blood, Ma pulled them off and told Ben to take them away. She made a fresh poultice of oatmeal, crushed apples, and comfrey leaves and bound it to John's shoulder with clean linen strips. He groaned with each movement.

"Could thee eat some supper?" she asked.

"Just water," he whispered.

Cradling his head in the crook of her elbow, she held the tin cup to his lips. "Now sleep," she told him. "Thee should feel better in the morning."

He sank back onto the pillows, resting more quietly.

While we washed up, Ma made a pot of chicken soup for John, setting the trammel low onto the flames. Sheba had set out bread, cheese, a crock of mixed pickles, a bowl of blackberries, and a jug of buttermilk. We took our places on either side of the long plank table. What an ordinary thing to do, but it felt wonderful to be home again!

As the food was passed, I relaxed all over. After all those weeks in strange surroundings, I felt solid in my family's presence. Here I knew who I was and what was expected. I wondered how John would feel with our family.

Then I realized Sheba was talking about him.

"Can we save him, Ma?" she asked.

"I hope so. We should know by morning."

Ben was bursting with questions. "Tell us about thy trip. Did thee see soldiers? Were there Indians and Frenchmen? Did thee see a battle? How did you meet John McCowen?"

But Will said, "Let them eat in peace, Ben. They are home safe now, and that's all that really matters. Table talk should be Holy Conversation. They can tell us only gossip and adventures. Surely thee can wait for idle stories."

I felt stifled. The whole trip had been about God's world, God's ways, God's expectations of his people. Why wouldn't telling about it be Holy Conversation? But no one ever won an argument with Will. Out of recent habit, I looked over at Enoch for his reaction. He gave me a wink. So I just passed it on to Ben, and he understood I would tell him our stories later.

By the time we finished supper, Ma's soup was ready. She took a bowl of it to John and found him half awake. The broth seemed to revive him, and he ate some chicken as well. But even chewing wore him out.

Ma said, "Sheba, bring some water from the well. Thee and I will tend John through the night. We will change the compresses, feed him soup, and give him sips of water every hour or so. I think he will be better in the morning."

Enoch had taken the wagon to the barn and unhitched the horses. He would spend the night with us, and then first thing in the morning he and I would take John's pelts into Philadelphia and collect our twelve pounds from Benjamin Franklin. Enoch wanted money in his pocket before he went home to Deborah.

We took Pa and Will and Ben to look at the pelts in the wagon barn.

"These are fine bear skins," Pa said. "Panther, lots of deer, beaver, fox, muskrat. He's done a good job stretching and scraping. These should fetch top prices. Beaver will bring the best price, no doubt. Here's my offer. For room and board and nursing care here until he's able to manage on his own, I'll take two of his bear skins."

"If John has any sense, he'll agree to it, Pa," Enoch said.

"The rest will bring a small fortune. Twenty-five per cent of it will be yours, besides the twelve pounds from Franklin. Not bad for a few weeks' labor, and an adventure as well."

I noticed Pa said not a word about a hare-brained idea. I guess we did all right.

"Where should we take them, Pa?" I asked.

"Friend Mifflin is about to send a ship to England, so he may want fur. His store is next to the drawbridge, opposite Hamilton's wharf."

"Thanks, Pa. We'll leave at first light tomorrow.

That night, the full moon once more filled our bedroom as Ben and I got ready for bed. Ben couldn't wait any longer to hear about the trip. "Tell me all about it, Noble," he insisted.

I hesitated. I could tell him about Peter's wagon going over the side of the mountain and about the murdered family, about finding John and rescuing Broken Blade. But the most important part was what I'd thought about, what I'd learned. How could I explain all that?

Suddenly I was very tired. "Maybe tomorrow, Ben," I mumbled.

"I knew it! Thee has become a man, and thee treats me like a child!"

I was startled. A man should know what he believes. A man should have his own tools and a job. How did

Ben think I had changed? But, still, a sense of accomplishment welled up inside me. I had felt the same way when my master had approved my apprentice piece table.

Then I smiled a secret smile. If Ben was right, it would be manly to tell the child a story.

"All right," I began. "We met the wagon train at the wharves in Philadelphia and spent the first night at The White Horse Inn."

CHAPTER 14

Settling Up

My mind outraced the team clopping along to Philadelphia. Today we would be paid twice, once from Benjamin Franklin and second from John McCowen. At last I could buy tools.

As we neared the city, I said to Enoch, "Look how the farms are shoulder to shoulder along here, no forests between."

"Aye," Enoch replied.

"The farms look smaller than ours."

"They've probably divided them for acreage for their children."

"Will Pa do that?"

"Pa's grand scheme is to apprentice each of us to a different trade for extra income in the off seasons and to keep us working for him. He'll buy about 200 acres for each of us, but he won't transfer titles until he dies because he says, 'Thee can never be sure how people will turn out.' He expects us to go along with his plan, hoping to outlive him. I'll have nought to do with it, myself. I won't let him run my life."

That was the longest speech I'd ever heard from Enoch.

Enoch had refused an apprenticeship. I remembered his fierce Quakerly arguments with Pa about that, full of shouts followed by stony silences. Then Enoch married Deborah. Her father had died, and her mother needed Enoch's help on their farm.

Pa had been quick to tell Will and Ben and me, "Look at Enoch! Working for someone else, no backup trade to turn to. Mark my words, lads, he'll crawl to me for help one day."

Will had inherited Pa's knack for making money in unexpected ways and already had some out on loan. I had learned woodworking, and Ben was about to apprentice to a blacksmith. But Pa expected all of us would first of all be farmers.

Not me. I loved the smooth fine grain of cherry, the hard rough ridges of oak, the fragrance of red cedar. I had fun filling the floor with wooden curls peeling off a plane and then kicking through them. I was proud of turning square sticks into round spindles with a drawknife. The whine of the lathe was my favorite music. I knew I could earn a year-round living by the skill of my hands, if I could only get a job.

Back on the farm, I felt like a little boy again, no matter what Ben thought. I did a man's work but wasn't drawing a man's pay. And I worried about forgetting my woodworking skills.

But this day I would buy some of the tools I needed. Then I would make a fine chair or small table to show when I asked for journeywork. My hands were itching for the feel of wood and tools. I began making a list in my head: saws, a miter box, planes, hammers, drawknives, brace and bits, chisels, files.

The commotion of Philadelphia was a little unsettling after a month of near silence in the Back Counties.

Enoch must have thought so, too. He sat straight and held the reins firmly.

At the wharf, I saw crowds of immigrants like Horst and his family. Many had toolboxes. What kind of future would they have?

Enoch drove directly to the warehouse where we were to be paid. The clerk told us the wagon train hadn't arrived yet. We should come back later in the day.

"Let's go on to Mifflin's store and unload John's pelts," I said.

"All right, but thee cannot spend any of John's money today," Enoch reminded me. "We must give him the whole amount and let him give us our share himself."

"Yes, but I can look at tools at Mifflin's, and we can go back after we get our pay for the trip. I can spend that money today, at least."

Enoch rolled his eyes. "I'll stay with the wagon. Thee may go inside, since thee can't wait."

Jonathan Mifflin's store was a three-story brick building filling a double lot. Three windows with small panes dimly lit the crowded stockroom. The front and back doors stood open to let in more daylight.

The walls were lined with floor-to-ceiling shelves filled with stuff I didn't want. Long tables in the middle of the floor held lots more. Along one wall, the shelves were stocked with spices--cloves, ginger, mace, cinnamon, and nutmeg. Tins of teas, pepper, and coffee glistened in the dim light. Barrels of preserved beef, pork, and mackerel crowded the aisles and filled the store with a vinegary smell.

I wandered to the back where iron pots and skillets

dangled from racks. There on one counter and the shelves behind it were all the tools I coveted.

Then I sneezed, my nose overwhelmed by the strong scents and pungent odors. At the sound, Jonathan Mifflin looked up from his ledger and said, "May I serve thee, young Friend?"

"My brother is outside with a wagonload of pelts from the Back Counties. Our pa told us thee might be interested in them."

"And who is thy father, lad?"

"Noble Butler of Goshen Meeting in Chester County."

"Thy father is correct. I might be interested in them. Let me have a look."

I took him out to the wagon. We folded back the tarp and uncovered John's bales.

Mifflin's eyes widened. "And how came thee upon such a load as this?"

I had thought he might think these were stolen goods. The truth was so unusual as to be nearly unbelievable. It was good Pa had sent us to a Quaker. Dealings among Quakers were always based on honesty.

I said, "Coming back from the supply trip to Wills's Creek, we found a wounded man in the road. We offered to take him with us, but he wouldn't leave without his pelts. So I unloaded them out of his cave where he had been trapping since early last winter. Now he's at our plantation, under our mother's care, and he commissioned us to sell the furs for him."

"Ah, yes. I heard that the wagoners are to return today from that supply trip. These pelts appear to be very fine, indeed." Turning to Enoch, Mifflin said, "If thee would drive thy wagon around behind the store, we will weigh and evaluate the lot of them to set a fair price."

Mifflin called two of his clerks, who unloaded John's pelts in the brick courtyard behind the store. One clerk used a large balance scale with arms of equal length. At the end of each arm a trio of chains suspended a wide pan. On one pan he placed the pelts, and on the other a collection of weights to balance them. We knew that such scales had passed inspection and weighed true. The other clerk wrote the contents, weight, and price on two pieces of paper.

Then Mifflin took the papers, added the columns, thought a minute, and said, "The going rate is £1 per pound for beaver, bear, muskrat, fox, otter, raccoons, sables, lynx, and wildcats. These weigh sixty-two pounds. For buckskin, the rate is one Spanish dollar each. Thee has brought in four bucks. So the total is £62 and four Spanish dollars."

We shook hands with Mifflin to seal the bargain. Then he counted out coins from his till and put them, along with one of the inventory papers, in a leather drawstring bag for us.

"Thank thee very much, Friend," I said. "John McCowen will be pleased."

"I thank *thee*, young Friends. One of my ships leaves on Second Day next on the outgoing tide, and I am happy to send these skins on to Friends in England."

Enoch stuffed the pouch of coins inside his shirt, where it rested atop his belt. As we drove away, Enoch said, "Seventy-five percent for John comes to a little over £46. And for us, add our share to the pay for the supply trip, and we'll have almost a year's wages. Now back to the warehouse. Surely the wagoners will be there by now."

"There they are!" I exclaimed. "Look! They are just arriving."

And there were all the wagoners, looking forward to their £12, as Franklin promised.

Franklin himself came out to meet us, a sheaf of papers in his hand. "Welcome back, and thanks to all of you. The entire colony of Pennsylvania and the Crown of England salute you for your bravery and generous gift of your time. The good news is that General Braddock's army is now well supplied. The bad news is that General Shirley has not yet sent the money to pay you."

I couldn't believe my ears. All my hopes were dashed. "Nay!" I shouted. "Nay! After five long weeks thee cannot deny us our wages!" I felt my face flush. I stamped my foot and shook a fist in the air. "We've earned that money! Thee *promised*!"

The other wagoners forgot their own anger and stared at me. Enoch tried to quiet me, but I shook him off.

"We risked our very lives," I ranted. "We thought thee sent us out in good faith! Go home and wait for our pay *some other day*?! If not today, how can we trust thee for another?"

I heard Daniel mutter, "I knew those Quakers went only for the money. They make a dollar any and every way they can, and they expect the rest of us to believe they're so holy."

"Noble, settle thyself!" Enoch shook me by the shoulders.

That brought me to my senses. I looked around and realized I was making a spectacle.

Shame engulfed me. I ducked my head and pushed through the crowd back to the wagon.

From there, I heard other wagoners take up my complaint with yells of their own.

"But wait," Franklin said, holding up a hand to quiet them. "I have here papers for each of you certifying that you have made the trip in good faith, and when the money comes from General Shirley, I will put a notice in the *Pennsylvania Gazette*. Bring these papers back with you, and you will be paid at that time."

"Men," Jedediah spoke up, "These papers will count as letters of credit in many places. You *will* be compensated. And we will meet again then."

Jedediah and Franklin handed out the papers. Enoch claimed ours and then came to find me. I was pacing around the wagon, head down, hands clasped behind my neck in despair.

"Franklin is a business man, Noble, a man of his word. But he's handling this transaction through the British government. He can't pay all of us out of his own pocket. He's given us vouchers to use for credit until the money comes in. Surely we'll be paid eventually."

"Eventually! Indeed! I won't ask Jonathan Mifflin for credit. I can't spend John's money, and after five long weeks, I have none of my own. So today, the day I've looked forward to for two whole months, I go home with no tools."

"Why is thee in such a hurry for tools anyway? Thee can always make a living farming."

I just glared at him. He would never understand.

"Let's just go home," I mumbled. I had nothing more to say for miles.

Finally my seething and shame settled to melancholy. By the time we got home, I had glumly accepted that I would just have to wait. Who knew how long? At least I would have some money from John's pelts.

As we rounded the last curve, there was Ben perched atop the snake fence, waving his floppy-brimmed straw hat. Enoch slowed the horses, and I reached an arm to help Ben swing himself into the wagon. Just seeing Ben made me feel a little better.

Ben had all kinds of questions about John McCowen. I could only say, "We don't know much about him. His family lived on the Juniata River, where the worst violence has been. He's been told they've gone to Easton, so no doubt he'll go looking for them when he's able."

"Ma says that won't be any time soon."

"Then we'll hear his stories, if he's willing to tell them."

We found John sitting up in his bed in the parlor. "How does thee fare, John?" I asked.

"I've been tended by an angel through the day," John smiled in Sheba's direction. "She fed me, gave me sips of water, and sang me sweet songs. Whatever thoughts I might have had of dyin', she pulled me back."

Sheba blushed. She didn't seem to know what to do with her hands. She pushed stray wisps of hair up under her cap, she plucked at her apron, she fidgeted with her pocket.

"Here, Sheba," Ma rescued her. "Put this platter of biscuits on the table and get the honey pot from the hutch."

Enoch dropped the leather pouch onto the linen sheet. "There's the pay for thy pelts, John. I think thee will be pleased. Count it out and give us our twenty-five percent."

John fumbled with the tightly drawn laces and then shook a shower of English pounds and Spanish silver dollars onto the coverlet. There were whole dollars, semi-circled halves, and wedge-shaped quarter coins with milled edges so anyone could tell the silver had not been shaved. And there with the coins was the receipt from the merchant, detailing the purchase. It all added up to an honest transaction.

John beamed as he counted the coins. "Thank thee kindly. This is more money than I've ever seen at one time. For sure Mr. Crogan would not have paid me this much."

I held out my hand for my share. It was good to have *some* pay for this long trip.

CHAPTER 15

The Longest Summer

Everything at home somehow looked smaller. On the trip to Wills's Creek I had seen bigger farms than ours. I had met people who knew more than Pa about a lot of things. I had seen the edge of the western world, and here I was back home in Chester County, doing the same old things, nowhere closer to my goals, and my head was still full of unanswerable questions.

But Pa wouldn't let me sit around thinking. Not Pa.

"Noble, I want you and Ben to move the snake fence from the east pasture to the west field. The sheep have gnawed the grass down to bare soil, and we've got to move them before the next rain washes the whole pasture down to the creek."

So Ben and I hitched Hope to the old farm wagon and drove to the east pasture. Pa had already moved the sheep into the barnyard so we could get the job done quickly. We began dismantling the rails that crisscrossed each other at angles. I lifted the top rail off and threw it in the wagon, then the next one and the one after that, working my way down the field.

"Why is it called a snake fence?" Ben asked. "Any snake could get through this pile of rails."

I couldn't believe my ears. Was he joking, or did he really not know?

"It's not to keep out snakes. It just *looks* like a snake. Don't you see how it wiggles alongside the lane?"

"Oh." Ben's voice sounded small. He hated it when someone pointed out the obvious to him. To make up for it, he climbed onto the top rail and, holding his arms out straight for balance, teetered his way from one cross-point to the next. At the end, he jumped down, feeling better about himself.

I envied him at that moment. I wished I felt better about myself. Instead of balancing my way down a narrow rail and landing firmly on the ground, I was figuratively *sitting* on the fence. Would I jump down on the farm side or on the lane that led to the city? Would I keep on doing what Pa wanted me to do, or would I have the means and the courage to become a cabinetmaker? In other words, would I be Pa's hired hand the rest of my life, or would I become my own man? I couldn't even see the way clear to stand up and get to the end of the rail the way Ben had. I felt glued to the fence.

"Come on, Ben. Let's get the job done. No time for play." I sighed. I had just sounded exactly like Pa.

The rest of that summer of 1755, there were only two things that took my mind off the drudgery of farming: watching John recover and fall in love with my sister, and worry about what was going on out west. Will and Ben and I swung sickles and pulled flax and chopped and hauled wood as if it were any other ordinary summer. But my thoughts were with General Braddock's army and Fort DuQuesne.

The first week John was with us, he spent most of

each day in bed. Every morning he was somewhat stronger than the day before, but his fever returned every evening. Although Ma supervised, Sheba became his regular nurse, and Ben became his shadow.

One hot day, Ben and I were taking a break from hoeing corn. I could tell there was something on his mind. Finally he said, "When Sheba tends our cuts and bruises, we want to get right back to whatever we've been doing. But John is different. He surely wants to recover, but he seems in no big hurry about it."

"Why?"

"When she changes his bandage, he seems to relish her touch."

"Oh? How can thee tell?"

"He sort of arches into her hands like a cat being petted. And if she hurts him even a little, he yells out. He seems to enjoy her apology. I think either John is a big baby or he's playing some sort of game with her."

"Keep watching, Ben. We'll sort this out." I smiled to myself. I knew the game.

The next week John joined Ben and me in the field, doing what he could with one hand. When Sheba thought he had done enough, she came to coax him back.

"John, thee must not overdo! Come to the house and rest a while."

And John followed her, docile as a lamb.

"Look at that!" Ben said. "She'll give him a mug of cider, and they'll sit under the sycamore and talk. I wish I could hear what they say."

That evening John hunkered down in the doorway to watch us at work. Ma and Sheba were spinning wool. I was carving a piece of poplar for the chair I was making. Will sharpened saws and scythes, and Ben tried to break a colt to harness.

On the bench by the well, Pa was lacing together two pieces of leather with waxed linen thread, making a shoe.

"Be ye a cordwainer, then?" John asked, watching Pa intently.

"Aye," Pa answered.

"I apprenticed for that trade once," John said softly.

"And did thee finish the apprenticeship?"

"Nay, after the Great Burnin', my master went one way, and we went another."

Ben opened his mouth to ask about the Great Burnin', but Pa's warning glance silenced him. I was sure I'd hear about it later.

That night after we went to bed, Ben asked me, "Does thee know about the Great Burnin' John mentioned?"

"Aye. His family was burned out of their home in the west. They weren't the only ones. A whole settlement was burned. I saw the ruins. It was awful."

"Was it an accident?"

"No! The Assembly sent men to evict the families because they had settled on Indian land. The government was trying to appease the Indians, but they weren't satisfied even with that, I guess."

"That's terrible! But it explains why his master went one way and he went another."

"And why John doesn't want to talk about it. That's the reason Pa cut thee off."

"Maybe John could finish his apprenticeship with Pa. Then we could keep him here longer," Ben ventured.

Finally John's fever left for good. One afternoon while Ben and I were fishing for trout in the creek, he asked, "Has thee noticed how strange Sheba is acting lately?"

"What does thee mean?"

"She helped John walk to the bench by the well. Surely he needs no help walking. The wound is in his shoulder, not his leg! But John's arm was over her shoulder, and her arm was around his waist."

I couldn't help grinning. "Yes, I've noticed. And has thee seen how his eyes follow her around the kitchen?"

"Aye. What does it mean?"

" I think they are falling in love."

"John and Sheba?"

"Aye, I think so."

"Why would he love *her*?" Ben had never thought of Sheba as a woman.

"Why not? She's comely enough, and she certainly has been kind to him. He's seen no other girls for all those months he was on the mountain, trapping."

"Do Ma and Pa know?"

"I'm not sure. But if we've figured it out, likely they have, too."

"Would they let Sheba marry him and go live on the frontier?"

"I don't know. Mayhap when John is well, he'll leave and we'll never see him again."

Ben didn't like that possibility. "Mayhap Pa will let him stay here. We could use another hand on the farm."

That evening Pa brought home the *Pennsylvania Gazette* with news that once again changed our lives. He read it aloud at the table.

"Extract of a Letter from an Officer; dated at Fort Cumberland, July 18, 1755.

"The 9th Instant we passed and repassed the Monongahela, by advancing first a Party of 300 Men, which was immediately followed by another of 200. The General, with the Column of Artillery, Baggage, and the main Body of the Army, passed the River the last Time about 1:00. As soon as the whole had got on the Fort Side of the Monongahela, we heard a very heavy and quick Fire in our Front; we immediately advanced in order to sustain them; but the Detachment of the 200 and 300 Men gave Way, and fell back upon us, which caused such Confusion, and struck so great a Panick among our Men, that afterwards no military Expedient could be made use of that had any Effect upon them. The Men were so extremely deaf to the Exhortations of the General, and the Officers, that they fired away, in the most irregular Manner, all their Ammunition, and then run off, leaving to the Enemy the Artillery, Ammunition, Provision and Baggage; nor could they be persuaded to stop till they got as far as Gist's Plantation, nor there only in Part, many of them proceeding as far as Col. Dunbar's Party, who lay six Miles on this Side....

"The General had five Horses killed under him, and at last received a Wound through his Right Arm into his Lungs, of which he died the 13th Instant. Secretary Shirley was shot through the Head; Capt. Morris wounded. Mr. Washington had two Horses shot under him, and his Clothes shot through in several Places, behaving the whole Time with the greatest Courage and Resolution. Sir Peter Halket was killed upon the Spot. Col. Burton, and Sir John St. Clair wounded; and enclosed I have sent you a List of the Killed and

Wounded, according to as exact Account as we are yet able to get.'"

Pa's jaw was set, his countenance grim. Will and Ben stared straight ahead, ashen-faced and wide-eyed. Ma buried her face in her hands. Sheba's shoulders heaved with silent sobs.

I shuddered, thinking of the dead and broken bodies of a whole army. I had had so much faith that General Braddock's army would teach those Indians a lesson. But with the army defeated, who could stop them from attacking wherever they chose? Would they come this side of the Susquehanna? Was our family in danger?

And what would this mean for Peter? For all the rest waiting at the fort? Had Molly's Charley been killed? What would she do?

John's harsh brogue broke the silence. "Ye cowardly Quakers are to blame for all this death and destruction! We've begged your Assemblymen, but they refuse to let us raise a militia. And now you Quakers have the blood of all these brave soldiers on yer hands. *This did not have to happen*!" He banged his clenched fist on the table, rattling plates.

His sudden violence made us all jump. No one had ever confronted us like this. We could only stare at him or stare at our plates.

The force of John's anger depleted his strength. He slumped forward, crying with frustration and rage. Will and I helped him back to bed.

None of us knew what to say. We went silently about our chores, stunned by the news and by John's outburst.

At bedtime that night, Ben whispered to me, "Is John right, Noble? *Are* we to blame?"

How could I answer? I hadn't stopped worrying about having saved one Indian's life. If I were responsible for the death of anyone Broken Blade might kill, I suppose Quakers, at least those in the Assembly, might be responsible for the deaths of Braddock and his army.

"I don't know," I mumbled.

Next morning John came into the kitchen as we ate breakfast. He wore an air of determination we hadn't seen before. He was calm and polite as he said, "I'm off for Easton to find me family."

Sheba jumped to her feet, her hand to her mouth.

John ignored her and said to Pa, "Sir, I apologize for me outburst yesterday. I thank ye for allowin' me to stay. When I've found me family and set me life in order, I'd like to return. Yer daughter . . ." he cleared his throat and started again. "Yer daughter has captured me heart. I'd like to come again to see her. And the rest of ye, as well!" he hastily added.

"I hope no promises have been made, but thee is always welcome here," Pa replied. "Safe journey. We'll hold thee in the Light as thee looks for thy family."

John turned to Ma, "I thank ye kindly for takin' such good care of me, ma'am. My arm's near as good as ever."

Ma twisted a corner of her apron. She seemed as bewildered as I felt. "I'm glad thee has mended so well, John."

He shook hands with Will. Then he slapped me on the shoulder and said, "Ye saved me life, friend, and here I've found reason to keep on livin'. If ever I can return the favor, I'm yer man."

He tousled Ben's hair and then with a rough knuckle tipped his chin up. "Look after yer sister for me, Ben. I'm countin' on ye for that."

Ben nodded and then turned quickly away. His eyes were filling with tears that he hoped no one would notice.

"Sheba," John said with a winsome smile, "would ye walk wi' me down to the road?"

And so John walked out of our house, but not out of our lives.

CHAPTER 16
A New Job

Summer dragged on, my spirits low. The trip to Wills's Creek had been a waste of time. General Braddock was dead, and no one had convinced those heathen redskins that they mustn't murder settlers. Lots more people had been killed, soldiers and settlers.

What was left of the world beyond Chester County now? Had McDowells finished their stockade, and would it hold up under attack? I wondered what had become of Peter, of Molly and her Charley. Had John found his family? Most of all, I feared what Broken Blade was doing and whether I was accountable for his actions.

The more I gnawed on these worries, the more I wished I had just stayed home. I had nothing to show for the trip but agony. I still had no tools, no prospects. I fell into bed every night too tired to dredge up hope for a better future.

Then one day in the middle of Tenth Month, I came from the fields into the kitchen and found Pa reading the latest *Pennsylvania Gazette*. He looked over his spectacles and said, "Son, thee must go to Philadelphia tomorrow. Franklin is ready to pay the wagoners who went to Wills's Creek. It's obvious he's no farmer. City folk know nothing about harvest time."

I could scarce believe my ears. Hope sprang up like a shoot from a forgotten seed.

"At last! I'm more than happy to go. Is Enoch going?"

"Nay, he can't take the time. He asks thee to bring him his share."

My excitement faded. "Even with my half, I still won't be able to buy all the tools I need."

"But thee can buy a few. I can't spare a horse, so hitch a ride from someone at Trimble's store."

The next morning I found a ride with a woman and her daughter taking produce into Philadelphia. I had a lot on my mind, so after the usual pleasantries, I kept a Quakerly silence.

I hoped I would see Christopher, because if anyone could answer my questions about Broken Blade, he could. Would Peter be there? And Molly? No, not Molly. As a tag-along woman she would collect no pay from the trip. But Peter might know about Molly's Charley. If Charley had been killed, would she claim my promise to be her friend? What would that mean?

I had really tried not to think of Molly, but it was impossible to forget her. Watching Sheba and John fall in love had brought a sense of emptiness into my own life. Oh, I had shared picnics after Quaker meeting for worship with one or another of the girls I had grown up with. I had even stolen kisses and given a few teasing pinches, but I had never gone courting.

At meetings over that summer, I had sneaked looks at girls. Some of them smiled back at me, others ignored me. They all seemed uninteresting, even ones I had thought attractive before my trip to Wills's Creek. I tried to think of them romantically, but I couldn't. Now, bouncing along in the wagon to Philadelphia, I realized why. I had been comparing them to Molly.

I pounded my forehead with the heel of my hand. Stupid! Stupid! Molly was in love with Charley, and besides, her ways were so different from ours.

Yet that made her even more exciting. She often popped up in my dreams as she had in the flesh on the trip to Wills's Creek. I always woke up discontented, frustrated.

I did admire her spirit and courage. If I could find a good Quaker girl with Molly's spunk and gumption, that would be the one for me. I wanted the joyful excitement I saw in John and Sheba's eyes.

About noon, we reached the High Street Market, and I arranged to meet my ride mid-afternoon for the return trip. Then I ran to the quay where the wagoners were to meet.

The first familiar face I saw was Daniel, grumbling as usual about politics and about having waited so long for his pay. There was good-hearted Horst. And Christopher!

I worked my way toward him through the crowd and stood at his elbow while he finished talking with another one of the wagoners. Finally he turned to me.

"Hullo, Noble," Christopher said. "Good to see you again."

"Aye, thee, too. Has thee been here long, or just arrived from the Back Counties?"

"I just came in, and barely in time to save my skin. The wilderness is full of bloodshed these days, and now settlers distrust me as much as the tribes do. Each side thinks I'm working for the other."

"What will thee do now?" I asked.

"Stay in Philadelphia and look for work as a translator, either for the government or the traders, whoever will pay for my services."

"By the way," I tried to sound casual, "has thee seen Broken Blade or heard of him?"

"Nay, but fierce as he is towards whites, he's bound to be part of the war parties attackin' settlers."

My heart sank. "I couldn't leave him pinned on the edge of that cliff. I had to free him. But ever since, I've worried that I'm responsible for the murders he might commit."

"Can't help you with that one, Noble. I never did understand Quaker reasoning. You'll just have to live with the consequences of being true to your beliefs."

Someone shouted, "Noble!"

I swung around, and there was Peter!

"Peter! I thought thee might still be in the militia!"

"Nay, I signed up for just three months. Remember Molly? Her Charley was killed in the battle for Fort DuQuesne, and now she and I are married."

Jealousy stabbed deep in my gut. Molly and Peter! Peter, in the right place at the right time, when Molly was grief-stricken over Charley's death. Peter, no older than me, already married! And all this in less than four months!

"Why, Peter!" I stammered. "Best wishes!"

Then I felt a rueful relief. I'd always known Molly was not right for me. Now she was Peter's wife. But would she leave me alone in my dreams? I hoped so!

I asked, "Does thee live in the city now?"

"Nay, we live near Easton, on the farm with Pa. And come spring we'll be havin' a baby."

"That's wonderful, Peter," I didn't know what else to say.

"Aye, we think so. That's another reason I'll be happy to collect this pay today. Mr. Franklin is making good the loss of my wagon and team, and then I can pay off Molly's indenture here in the city. I'm trying to make an honest woman of her," Peter grinned. "If ever you come to Easton, Noble, you'd be more than welcome to stay with us."

"Thanks, Peter. I'll remember that."

Benjamin Franklin appeared in the doorway with a tray stacked with coins. Jedediah, standing beside him, called out the names of the wagoners one by one as Franklin handed each of us British coins of the realm. I saw Daniel count his carefully. Then he checked the edges to be sure they were full value sterling silver. Horst held open his pouch and watched the glittering coins pour in, his red face beaming.

I was hoping Franklin would not remember my outburst last time. I had a little speech ready. When he handed me my pay, I said, "Thank thee kindly, Friend. I am grateful not only for the money but also for the trip itself. We supplied the army, but the trip supplied me with experiences and ideas I'll not forget."

Franklin's eyes were intense behind his spectacles. His look pinned me to the spot as he said, "This money will soon be spent, I'll wager, but your experiences and ideas will last much longer. Use them wisely, young man."

"Thank thee. I'll do my best."

Once I had my pay, I hurried to Jonathan Mifflin's store to buy some tools at last. Mifflin looked up and nodded as he recognized me. "Has thee brought me another load of pelts, young Friend?"

"Nay, I've come to spend this time. I'd like to look at woodworking tools." I took the crumpled list out of my pocket although I knew it by heart. "First I need a brace and some bits and then a plane. How much would they cost?"

"We have some fine planes from England, just off the ship. They start at £6."

"Does thee have a brace and bits?"

"Aye, fine ones from the Low Countries. A brace is £5, and bits are £1 apiece.""

That little sprout of hope withered. I didn't have enough for even my basic list. "I'll buy the brace and one bit today, and I'll buy more later as I can."

Then on impulse I asked Mifflin, "Does thee know of any jobs for woodworkers in the city? I've finished my apprenticeship in Chester County but can find no journeywork without tools of my own."

Mifflin thought for a moment. "Most cabinetmakers engage indentured servants who come from the Old Country with their own tools and years of experience, I think."

I guess my disappointment touched his heart, because then he asked, "Would thee consider another kind of job? Israel Pemberton said only yesterday that he might hire a runner. It's not woodworking, but thee would have room and board and a small wage. There might even be tips. Thee would become acquainted with leading people in the city and might hear of a job as thee accumulates tools."

"What is a tip?"

"It's a gratuity, 'To Insure Promptness.'"

"Who is Israel Pemberton?"

"He is a weighty Quaker devoted to peace."

"Aye, I would be interested in any honorable way to earn money for tools. Where might I find Friend Pemberton?"

"He lives at Third and Chestnut, just around the corner. His house is surrounded by gardens, so thee will know it when thee sees it. Go to the side door, where his office is."

"Thank thee, Friend."

The feel of tools in my hands again and the chance to be on my own gave me courage. Whoever Israel Pemberton was and whatever a runner did, I was ready!

The Pemberton house was easy to find. It was brick, like most of the grand houses in the neighborhood, but this one had an amazing garden. Brick-lined gravel paths, shrubs shaped like cones and pyramids! At the far end was a fancy little house, but it had no walls. The sides were all open, and there were benches around the inside edges. It was all for show. If there were vegetables growing anywhere, I didn't see them. Trees were shedding bright leaves, but not a single leaf littered these walks. I could hear noise from High Street, but this garden seemed a world away.

I found the side door of the Pemberton house and carefully wiped the soles of my shoes on the boot scraper. Then I tapped the fancy door knocker.

An elderly man opened the door. “Good day,” he said pleasantly. “How may I help thee?”

“My name is Noble Butler. Jonathan Mifflin said Friend Israel Pemberton wanted a runner.”

“Hmm. Yes.” He seemed surprised, I thought. Then he smiled and said, “I’m Israel Pemberton. Come into my office here and have a seat.”

I tried not to gawk as we walked into a large room, but I had never been in such an elegant house. There was a patterned carpet on the floor. Venetian blinds hung at the two windows. Friend Pemberton seated himself in a Windsor chair at a mahogany secretary with brass pulls on the drawers, just the kind I hoped to make some day. The upper doors of mirrored glass had notes stuck into the frame. Pigeonholes and slots in the middle were stuffed with papers and account books. I had to wrench my eyes away from this piece of furniture so I could pay attention to Friend Pemberton.

He waved me to sit in a straight chair at another desk. Hanging above it was a rack of pigeonholes filled with papers of all kinds. Both the secretary and this little desk were cluttered with candleholders, inkstands, and jars of quill pens.

I sat stiffly on my chair, feeling awkward.

“Friend Mifflin knows how busy I am,” Pemberton said. “He suggested I employ a runner to deliver messages, do errands, be available for whatever was needed at a moment’s notice. Perhaps God has sent thee just when I need thee most. Thee would have room and board here, and I would pay thee a shilling a week. Does that interest thee, Noble?”

My thoughts raced. Out of the blue, here was an offer to move into the city! Friend Pemberton was offering wages, room and board. Surely I could save enough to buy the tools I wanted so badly. And mayhap I'd meet a cabinetmaker who could use me.

I tried not to sound too eager. "Aye, but I've never heard of such a job."

Friend Pemberton said in his dignified, city voice, "It's rather common for people in my circumstances to have a runner. Important matters in business and government cannot wait for postal delivery when a runner can carry a message and return with an answer in minutes. It is not a lifetime job, just one for a young person. My brother James has a runner named Tom who would train thee."

"I would be honored to serve thee, but I live in Chester County and barely know my way around Philadelphia."

Pemberton smiled. "Thee will learn quickly. William Penn, our Founder, planned the city in an easy grid from the Delaware River to the Schuylkill River. North-south streets are numbered, and east-west streets are named for trees. Could thee arrange to begin in two days? Thee would have time to get thy things together, say goodbye to thy family, and return the following morning. What think thee of that?"

"It suits me very well. I'd be glad to help thee."

"Good. Let's shake hands on it, then, and I'll see thee mid-morning two days hence."

Pemberton ushered me out the side door and closed it behind me. I thought I might explode with joy, but I tried to walk deliberately, slowly, back to High Street, biting my lip to contain this great excitement. Once out of sight of the Pemberton house, though, I threw my hat in the air and flung myself into cartwheels, shouting at the top of my voice, "I have a job! A real job!"

Then my elation fizzled when I realized what I would face at home. Pa would have a fit! This was harvest season, and he was counting on my help. But at last I had a chance to lead my own life! If I didn't take it now, I'd likely be stuck on the farm till I'd lost all my skills, living out Pa's grand plan and never doing what I myself wanted. However, Israel Pemberton had said perhaps God had sent me there. Mayhap it was God's plan versus Pa's plan. The thought made me smile again.

"A job in the city, Noble?" Pa asked. "Who has offered to hire thee, and to do what, exactly?" A storm was gathering in his voice.

"He wants a runner, Pa, someone at his beck and call to deliver messages all around the city. He's a very busy man."

"I'm a busy man, too, and I'm counting on thee to help bring in the harvest." I could hear his thunder coming. "A runner? Never heard of such a job. This isn't the kind of work thee has been hoping for. Why would thee want to do it?"

"Not for the rest of my life, surely. This is just a beginning job. By the time I can buy my tools, I hope to meet a cabinetmaker who will hire me."

"And who is this city man who knows so little of farming that he would take thee off at harvest time?" Pa's eyes flashed lightning.

I took a deep breath and stood my ground. "He is a friend of Jonathan Mifflin's, Pa. Israel Pemberton."

"Israel Pemberton?" The storm I was dreading suddenly disappeared. "*The* Israel Pemberton? Why didn't thee say his name at the beginning of this conversation, Noble?"

"Does thee know him? I've never heard of him before today." I was astonished by Pa's sudden turn.

"He is one of the richest men in Philadelphia, the weightiest Quaker of them all. He is clerk of the Philadelphia Yearly Meeting and runs all the Quaker schools. Not only is he a friend of Jonathan Mifflin, he's much involved with Benjamin Franklin. He helped Franklin organize the Library Company, the Fire Company, the Almshouse, and a lot of other enterprises in the city. Thee has fallen into a small job offered by a very big man. Only for Israel Pemberton would I permit thee to leave us at this time of year. Thee can work for him now, but I expect thee back for spring planting."

My eyes widened at all this news. I gulped and then said, "Thankee, Pa. A good thing, too, because I shook his hand on the job offer."

Pa grimaced. "That's exactly what I would have done myself. Well, we'll see how much work thee can do around here tomorrow before thee leaves."

The next day Pa had me working in the field from before sunup until after sundown harvesting Indian corn with Will and Ben. In the fading light my muscles ached, but my heart soared.

After supper that evening, Ma said, "Our family is shrinking! First Enoch left, and now thee, Noble. I am happy for thee to have this chance in the city, but we will miss thee sorely."

I beamed. In fact, I had hardly stopped smiling since Pa agreed to let me go. "I'll miss thee, too. But I can't wait to realize my dreams."

Will groaned, "Thee picks a fine time to leave. Harvest is the heaviest work of the year."

Pa brushed his complaint aside. "Thee forgets what a strapping lad Ben has become. If the three of us cannot handle the work, I'll hire someone. We'll manage, because Noble has a job with *Israel Pemberton*. A temporary job. He'll be back for spring planting."

CHAPTER 17

Israel Pemberton

The next day Israel Pemberton welcomed me inside and then, pulling a bell rope in his office, he summoned his other servants to introduce me to them. "This is Noble Butler, my new runner," he announced. "I'm sure each of ye will make him feel at home here and help him find his way as needed."

Everyone nodded and smiled.

"Noble, this is my *actual* butler, Ralph, from Wales," Pemberton said.

I ducked my chin, for the first time embarrassed by my family name.

"His wife Gwyneth is our cook. I'm sure thee will want to be on her good side. Bert here is the groom who cares for the horses, and his Betsy is our housekeeper. Thee will sleep with the other servants on the third floor."

Betsy led me toward narrow steps rising from the upstairs hallway. The third floor was a long central hall lined with six doors. The last room was mine. There was a single bed with linen sheets, woolen blankets, and piles of pillows. A room all to myself! I knew I'd miss Ben.

A row of pegs for hanging clothes lined the low wall under the sloping ceiling, and a dormer window overlooked the kitchen garden. So that's where the vegetables grew! I dropped my small bag on the bed.

"Friend Pemberton wants thee to wear these," Betsy said, handing me two sets of clothes and a black tricorn hat.

The dark knee breeches were of richer cloth than any I had seen back home. The two shirts were fine white linen. There was even a vest with shiny metal buttons and big pockets for all those notes I would deliver. Then she gave me a greatcoat with even larger pockets and buttons, white knee stockings, and leather shoes with metal buckles, like the ones Pa made for wealthy customers.

"Thank thee. I will try to do him credit," I said, feeling a bit overwhelmed.

Betsy waited outside my door while I changed clothes and then went on showing me around the house.

"Thee will take thy meals in the kitchen, and Gwyneth will show thee where to sit," she explained, showing me the cheerful kitchen. Two tables were set with woven cloths and surrounded by ladder-back chairs with seats of woven rushes. Gwyneth nodded and smiled at me as she rolled piecrusts on her long worktable.

"Tom, James Pemberton's runner, will go on errands with thee till thee learns thy way. Oh, here is Tom now."

The side door opened, and there was a lad much like Ben in age and size. He was dressed in the same sort of clothes Betsy had just given me. His pockets bulged with letters, and notes were stuck in the ribbon around his hat.

"Hullo, Noble," he said with a grin. "I hear thee will come with me on my rounds this afternoon."

Friend Pemberton came in just then, and Tom said, "Good day, Friend. Does thee have letters for me today?"

"Aye, Tom. Here's a stack of them. When thee returns, no doubt I'll have more."

So the two of us set out. Tom's good-natured commentary as we ran through alleys and streets together helped me learn more than just the geography of the city.

"There are three Pemberton brothers," Tom explained, "Israel, then James, then John. Israel and James ran the family business themselves until recently. They are very rich. But Israel decided business was taking too much time from what he most wanted to do."

"And what would that be?"

"To make Philadelphia truly the City of Brotherly Love. So for the past five years, he's been completely involved in public affairs. He and Benjamin Franklin became friends. Now he manages many of the causes he and Franklin started."

"So I must know where the schools are, and the hospital . . ." I said, remembering what Pa had said about Pemberton.

"And the homes of the other leaders involved in them," Tom finished for me. "I can show thee. I am sent to many of the same places."

"Has thee worked for James Pemberton a long time?"

"Since my mother died two years ago. My father died the year before, and James Pemberton rescued me from the Almshouse. He knew my parents through the Meeting and wanted me to have a home instead of growing up in the Almshouse. "

"Oh, Tom! I'm so sorry about thy parents. How long will thee be a runner? Does thee have other work in mind?"

"When James doesn't have me running, he has me studying. He thinks I could be a clerk in the family business in a year or so. God has been very good to me. If James hadn't taken me under his wing, I'd be in the Almshouse still."

I realized that Israel Pemberton might have taken a foundling from the Almshouse, too. I was glad he took a chance on me instead.

Each morning I was given a double handful of letters or notes to deliver. I carried messages to the Assembly House, some to the governor's office on the second floor, and others to the legislative chamber downstairs. I took packets to Benjamin Franklin's post office, many of them addressed to Friends in New Jersey, New England, or even London. I ran errands to Carpenters' Hall, where much business was done, although it was still being built, and to Quaker schools and the Almshouse.

It was easy to learn the numbered and tree-named streets. Winding alleys, muddy lanes, and private cut-throughs were another matter. But there was always someone to give directions. I ran from one destination to the next, and when I returned, there were always more papers waiting.

Israel Pemberton must be the busiest man in the city, I decided. This "runner" job was well named! Cobblestones are harder on shoes than farmland is, that's for sure, and city shoes didn't last as long as the boots Pa made.

Sometimes Friend Pemberton's correspondents didn't have time to write their replies, so they told me messages to take back. Those were the times when I earned tips of a penny or two. And through these messages I learned more about what was going on in the province as well as in the city.

Reports poured in about increased Indian attacks on settlers in the Back Counties. It seemed as if the tribes had waited until the British army was out of Pennsylvania, and then they felt free to attack wherever they chose. Of course I worried that Broken Blade was involved.

Philadelphia Quakers felt sorry for the settlers, but they weren't concerned for themselves. They couldn't believe the Indians would ever attack east of the Susquehanna. After all, on the east side of the river all the land had been paid for through treaties with the Six Nations and the eastern Delaware tribes.

Then on the 26th of Tenth Month, word came from Conrad Weiser, Pennsylvania's Indian agent, that people on the east side of the river had been massacred. John Harris, of Harris's Ferry where we crossed the Susquehanna on the way home, asked the Assembly to build a fort upriver to protect friendly Delawares. He knew that angry white settlers would seek revenge against any Indian.

By the end of Tenth Month, Weiser organized a militia with Governor Morris's permission and marched west, but when the militia heard of an attack on John Harris himself, they disbanded and went home to defend their families. Then Philadelphians began to worry. Almost every day, fleeing frontier families arrived in the city to take shelter with friends or relatives. They brought new reports detailing the horrors. The frontier was awash in settlers' blood and aflame with burning plantations, according to the *Pennsylvania Gazette*.

When I heard these reports, my mind churned. What if Indians attacked my family? Would I kill to keep them safe? Would that kind of killing be justified?

These questions would not leave me alone. Finally I decided to ask my master. As well-versed in Quaker teachings as he was, and as kind as he had been, mayhap he could give me some answers. After I finished my rounds one evening and found him at ease, I asked, "Would thee have time to answer some questions for me?"

"Aye, of course. How can I help thee?" he replied.

"Thee knows I'm a birthright Quaker, but with all the Indian attacks on settlers, I've wondered whether anyone can hold fast to nonviolent ways."

"Friends believe there is that of God within each person, Noble," he said, "Indians as well as whites, murderers as well as peace-loving Friends. We believe, and thee knows this thyself, that violence and especially killing are wrong."

"But if thee were attacked, what would thee do?"

"I would rather die than lift my hand in violence against one of God's children."

"Aye, thee would be ready to face death that way, and I hope I would as well, but what if thy family were in such danger? What would thee do then?"

"I would pray for their souls and for the souls of their attackers."

"Thee still would not lift thy hand?"

"I hope I would not."

"But these Indian attacks are terrible. I doubt I could stand by and see my family treated so."

"What they do *is* terrible, but, murderers though they be, they are still children of God, and for us to kill them, even to save our own, is a denial of what we know to be God's will."

"So I've been taught," I answered. "But if my family were threatened, I doubt I'd take time to think through what I'd been taught."

"There are Defense Quakers, who believe that in such cases it is permissible to suspend nonviolence. Has thee heard of them, Noble?"

"Nay. I've only been taught nonviolence."

"The problem with Defense Quakers is that they are being selective in deciding when to apply our principles. That's why they are dismissed from Meeting if they refuse to repent."

"But aren't they following the Light Within?"

"According to the teachings of our founder, George Fox, there is only one right thing to do, and the Light will reveal it. We may differ in our ability to discern the Light, and in our willingness to obey it. But his teachings are clear."

I nodded, but I still was not quite satisfied.

Pemberton went on, "Friends believe the best way to prevent violence is to deal fairly and kindly. The Delaware have been our friends ever since William Penn exchanged belts of wampum with them and promised to live in amity as brethren. They wouldn't be attacking now without cause. Instead of defending ourselves in a warlike manner, we should find the reasons for their disaffection and set things right. I suspect the Proprietors have not dealt honestly with them, and they see these attacks as their only recourse. In fact, this very issue is the subject of many of the messages I've had thee deliver in the past few days. The Assembly needs to inquire into this matter."

"But don't such inquiries take a long time? What of the settlers on the frontier while the Assembly investigates? Is their blood on the hands of the Assembly in the meantime?"

"Thee asks difficult questions, Noble," Pemberton answered with a wry smile. "I have no easy answers. But it seems urgent to do what we can here in Philadelphia to get to the root of the violence. I will never give up working for a peaceful solution with our Indian brethren. And thee is doing thy part as well. Tomorrow there will be another stack of letters for thee to deliver on this same topic. God speed you on your way."

As I carried messages around the city, I worried about my family. I worried about John McCowen. But most of all, I worried about what Broken Blade was doing. Was settlers' blood on my hands?

CHAPTER 18

Outside the Meeting

The icy wind off the Delaware River seemed to cut right through my fancy clothes as I waited outside the meeting house. My master was inside with other important Quakers talking about the impasse between the legislature and the governor. Deadly Indian attacks were shrinking the frontier closer and closer to Philadelphia. Could Friendly beliefs in peaceful ways meet this challenge?

Trying to keep warm, I paced between the meeting house and the shed for horses and carriages. I blew on my fingers and stamped my feet. It wasn't even winter yet, but already the ground was hard with frost. My eyes watered in the cold wind.

A crowd began to gather beyond the wall separating the meeting house from Front Street. I could hear angry voices but couldn't make out what they were saying. Then I saw a flatbed farm wagon driving slowly back and forth. I couldn't figure out what those strange things were on the wagon. I moved closer to see.

I could hear cries of disgust and mournful wails. And taunts!

"You Quakers are to blame for this!"

"Look on these victims and see if you can turn your fat backs again!"

Then I realized what the wagon carried: twisted corpses and separate body parts, some with their clothes torn off, victims of an Indian massacre. *Here,* in civilized Philadelphia!

I felt dizzy and sick. I braced myself against a tree and gulped cold air in quick deep breaths. Gradually my head began to clear, and I made myself look again. People were gathering from all directions. Their words were lost in shrieks of disgust and fury.

The wagoner drove slowly, deliberately, back and forth in front of the Meeting House. His knitted cap was pulled down over his ears and forehead. There was something familiar about that man.

Just then one of the wheels hit a pothole, jolting the wagon. Something flew off the back, and screams filled the air. The wagoner jerked on the reins and jumped down. Then he picked up what had fallen and held it high for all to see.

It was a man's severed arm, bent at the elbow, the fingers crooked. The bloody sleeve was still on it. The wagoner thundered at the crowd, "This was my friend Robert! Those bloodthirsty heathen hacked him to pieces in his lane. You Quakers, you who sit in safety and talk about peace, see what all your fine talk brings! Give us a militia to protect ourselves! It's too late for Robert here," he waved the arm again, "but unless you act soon, this could be your arm I'll be wavin."

The minute he spoke, I recognized him: John McCowen. He jumped back onto his wagon, still waving Robert's arm over his head.

Two men grabbed the reins from John's hand. Someone shouted, "Put these corpses on the steps of the Assembly Hall. All the legislators, not just the Quakers, need to see this!"

The crowd roared their approval. They surrounded the wagon and forced it up the street toward where legislators were in session.

I turned toward the meeting house and saw the Friends peering out the windows in disbelief. As I ran toward the door, Israel Pemberton came out to meet me.

"Noble, what's going on out there?"

Someone in the crowd threw a rock, just missing Pemberton's head. Another rock bounced off the front wall of the meeting house. We ducked inside and shut the heavy door just as a brick splintered window glass.

"A mob, upset by bodies of Indians' victims!" I stuttered. "They're headed for the Assembly Hall."

"And they blame us for the murders, don't they. The irony is that the Proprietors have brought these tragedies upon us, but they will pay naught in taxes to solve the problems they've created. Mark well the consequences of greed, Noble."

I stared at him. How could he talk politics at a time like this? Had he no feelings? Even if not moved by the dead bodies, had he no fear of the mob? Even *I* had a sense of what they could do.

Finally I found my voice. "This mob is apt to do damage at the Assembly Hall. They may even attack thy house before they finish."

Pemberton looked concerned, but he nodded calmly. Then he turned to the other men clustered nearby. "Friends, we have heard Noble's report. I suggest we return to our homes. If any of this mob comes to my door, I shall invite them in and endeavor to reason with them. Let us meet again tomorrow to consider further."

I couldn't believe my ears. Surely he should think twice before inviting that mob into his house. Or was he truly that brave, that he would risk the safety of his house and family to reason with them?

The Quaker leaders hurried off. We could hear breaking glass as the mob threw rocks at the Assembly Hall windows. Pemberton sent me to see if his brother James had returned to his own home nearby.

By the time I got there, the mob had unloaded the corpses across the main entrance to the Assembly Hall. They propped signs against the bodies, blaming legislators in general and Quaker legislators in particular for the murders. Assemblymen were escaping out the back door. Constables were dragging John McCowen toward the gaol at Third and High Streets, just a block away from our house.

I followed to see what would happen to John. Keeping in the background, I heard the gaoler charge him. "For disturbing the peace and inciting a riot, you must pay for damages done to the Assembly Hall."

John swore, "Yer Honor, I threw no rocks."

"But your actions led others to do so. Can you pay the damages?"

"I've no money, sir," John answered.

"Then you'll sit in gaol until someone pays your fine." The gaoler led him away, manacled.

Outside, constables were dispersing the mob. My head swam as I made my way back to Pemberton's house. How long would John have to sit in gaol? His family (if he had even found them) would have no way of knowing what had happened to him, and, even if they did, they probably couldn't bail him out. Poor John!

Then I thought of the bag of coins hidden under my mattress. I could bail him out. I was sure he would repay me when he could.

What a generous idea, my other self mocked. *And how long will that delay buying thy tools?*

I could picture each tool I so longed to own. I had memorized them at Mifflin's store and knew the price of every one of them. Now they seemed to fade beyond my reach.

I knew, too, that John would have to pay for his food or go hungry in gaol. I couldn't let him starve while I lived in comfort at Pemberton's house and saved money for tools.

He would repay me when he could, but he had no chance of earning money from a cell in gaol. Even if he didn't repay me for a long time, I could earn more money here in the city than John could in gaol.

But what would Friend Pemberton think of my freeing such a rabble rouser? Would he keep me on as his runner? If not, I'd be back on the farm in no time!

What if helping John ruined the chance to fulfill my dream? Surely that was asking too much in the name of friendship.

I decided I must tell Friend Pemberton and take that risk. How could I live with myself, knowing John was sitting in gaol just around the corner when I could have freed him? How could I ever face Sheba?

By the time I got back to the house, I knew what I had to do.

"Thy brother is safe," I reported. "He will call upon thee this evening."

"Thank God. And thank thee, Noble." Then, when I hesitated, Pemberton said, "Go on, what else?"

"The driver of the wagon has been arrested for disturbing the peace and fined the cost of damages to the Assembly building."

"That seems reasonable enough."

"Aye, it does. But he cannot pay the fine. He'll sit in gaol until the fine is paid somehow."

"That's the law, thee knows."

"The fact is, he's a friend of mine. I'd like to pay his fine with the money I've earned working for thee. I thought I should let thee know."

"Of course thee may use thy money as thee chooses. It's generous on thy part to use it thus. I know thee has in mind to buy tools."

"I'm sure he will repay me. But I didn't want thee to think I was working behind thy back."

"How does this man come to be thy friend, Noble? I understand from Isaac Norris that he comes from Northumberland County, near Easton."

So I told how we had brought John home with us and that he had left to find his family at Easton. Then I said, "I don't know how he came to drive that wagon into Philadelphia today. He didn't say those bodies were his family, but I've yet to hear his story."

"What an interesting young man thee is, Noble! Go rescue thy friend again. He can stay with thee tonight, and when thee has learned his adventures, I'd be glad to hear them myself." Pemberton smiled and dismissed me.

I hurried off to pay John's fees, including the release of his impounded wagon. John grinned broadly as we left the gaol.

"So now twice ye've come to me aid when I couldna' help meself! I'm forever in yer debt, me friend," he exclaimed. "I'll repay yer money as soon as I can get to me own, but repayin' yer kindness will take a lifetime. How in the world do ye happen to be in Philadelphia just when I needed a friend? And what's the news of yer family?"

I knew which family member particularly concerned John. "Thee can spend the night with me and we can talk. I want to hear how thee happened to be in Philadelphia today thyself."

"When I left yer farm that mornin', I headed for Easton," John began. "The first person I saw there turned out to be me father. I found the whole family, and we had a grand reunion."

"They were all safe, then?"

"Aye, but not together. Da works for Vernon, the ferryman. Mam cooks for Jacob Bachmann at his tavern. Me brothers, Duncan, Daniel, and Finlaw, each works for a different farmer in the area, so we're all scattered. But so far we're safe enough."

"Had they been attacked in Shearman's Valley?

"Nay, but their next neighbor's family was all murdered or stolen, and me mother lost all her nerve. She pleaded with me Da to take the family back east. He never could say no to her. If he'd had a legal claim to the land, I think he'd have dug in his heels. But he could see she was scared to death, and he thought to ease her mind. When he can get official papers, he'll go back to Shearman's Valley. Then no one will ever pry him off his land."

"And what does thee do, John?"

"I worked for Robert, a carpenter. We were buildin' the schoolhouse and helpin' various ones wi' their houses. Robert put me up in his barn, but last week Indians attacked him as he came home. Lucky for me I wasn't with him, or I'd be as dead as Robert."

"So now thee is looking for work?"

"Aye. I hang around Bachmann's Tavern talkin' to people who come in, hopin' to find a job. But what I'm findin', instead of work, is more stories of redskin attacks. I think soon we must have a militia, and I'll be the first one to sign up. We've got to stop these bloodthirsty heathen, or there'll be no decent folks left in Pennsylvania. When Finlaw's neighbors were attacked last week, most of 'em was killed and the rest stolen. And then Robert. Easton is in an uproar. People don't leave home without their guns, and families go everywhere together, leavin' no one behind, for fear of an Indian attack. We decided it was time to show the city folks what is goin' on upriver. So we loaded the bodies onto the wagon, and I drove them down. You know the rest of that story."

I nodded grimly. "What will thee do now?"

"Take the poor bodies home and let the neighbors give 'em a decent burial. I hope I've stirred the legislators enough to authorize a militia."

"Thee could go back to our farm. Pa's looking for help since I left, and I know Sheba'd be glad to see thee."

John stiffened. "Yer family was wonderful to me, Noble, and I love yer sister enough to make her me wife. But I won't go back until I can stand on me own two feet and make a good home for her. She knows that. I'm doin' me best, but these bloody savages have complicated everything. *We need a militia!*"

By this time, we had reached the Pemberton house. I arranged for John's horse to be stabled, and then we went into the kitchen. Gwyneth had saved a meat pie for us, and there were bowls of apples and nuts on the table as well.

John looked around appreciatively at the kitchen. I saw it through his eyes, spacious and clean. There were cotton curtains at the windows and white tablecloths. The tall ladder-back chairs were fancier than any he had seen before. "Ye've done well fer yerself, Noble," he commented. "How did ye git frae yer pa's farm to this fine house in the city?"

I briefly told my own story. As John listened, all friendliness drained from his face. He became stern, suspicious, angry.

"We're sittin' in the house of Israel Pemberton, leader of the Quakers? Noble, how can ye work for such a man? I canna stay here! I canna eat his food!" He thrust his chair backwards, toppling it onto the brick floor. Grabbing his cap, he rushed for the door.

"Wait, John!" I cried. "Don't leave!"

With one hand on the open door, John said over his shoulder, "If ye want to talk to me, then ye'll have to do it in the wide outdoors. I canna accept hospitality from such as Pemberton!" He stalked out without even a backward glance.

I was stunned by this reaction. Then I followed him through the gate out into the street. He stopped and turned abruptly. "Where's me horse and wagon? I'll be on me way."

"He's stabled for the night. I'll get him if thee insists. But, John, can't we talk? Why is thee angry with *me*?"

John paused before answering. Then he said more calmly, "Noble, as I said before, yer me friend for life. But how can ye work for a man who blocks defense for folks on the frontier? Just look around ye. Look at all this wealth and comfort. Yer boss may be a good man with the best intentions in the world. But he's responsible for the murders of good people who have no means, no permission even, to defend themselves. And if you accept his money and live in his house, you're benefittin' from his, his . . ."

He gave up looking for the right words and started over. "Noble, I know ye've been brought up in peaceful ways. But in these times, they just don't work! You saw those poor bodies in me wagon. What if they had been *your* people? Could you work for a man who kept them from protectin' themselves?"

John was so distraught that he could not stand still. He started pacing toward the river.

I did my best to keep up with him. John's words had pierced me. I had felt a vague disquiet in working for Pemberton, but I had never thought it through as clearly as John had just done.

By this time we had reached the harbor, and John strode out onto an empty pier. We sat silently on a couple of kegs under the frosty distant stars. Our breaths made little puffs of vapor.

After a while, I tried to explain. "Hear me out, John," I began. "Israel Pemberton isn't even a member of the Assembly. What could he do to stop the massacres on the frontier? In fact, how could he even block the Assembly from voting funds for a militia? How responsible can he be for what is happening?"

John spat contemptuously. "He's a leader of the Quaker Party! He has influence! What do you think is in those messages he has you carryin'? But he and his friends are unrealistic. That's why I brought those poor bodies to the city today, to give him and his ilk a good look at what's goin' on!"

"If he has influence," I said, "couldn't he use it to bring about peace? To correct the situation that leads to attacks on settlers?"

"How's he gonna do that? Give the redskins back their land? Then you'd have settlers attackin' *them*!"

"Well, what does thee think should be done, John?"

"I'll tell you what needs to be done! The Assembly needs to raise a militia and provide arms and ammunition to soldiers and settlers. Then they could defend themselves and wipe out the savages altogether. There'll be no peace as long as them heathen redskins hang around. They need to know we've a right to the land and move out of our way!"

"Well, thee hasn't convinced me it's wrong to work for Israel Pemberton. But thee has made me doubtful. Thee may be right—mayhap I should not be working for him. But I'm not ready to quit just yet. I still hope for a peaceful resolution."

By this time, John's anger had spent itself, and he was suddenly very tired. "Let's go get me horse and wagon from the stable. I'll tie up to a post here on the dock and sleep in the wagon. Then I'll collect the poor bodies and be off before dawn. "

We trudged back to Pemberton's stable and hitched up the sleepy horse. John clapped me on the shoulder. "Thanks again for bailin' me out. I'll repay ye soon as I can. I do know where to find ye," he said with a rueful smile. "And if ye come to yer senses and quit workin' for this Quaker, I'll get the money back to yer Pa's farm."

"Maybe, just maybe, John, Israel Pemberton will find the way to a peaceful settlement."

"Aye, when pigs can fly. Think hard about what I've said, Noble. Don't compromise yerself fer an easy job."

That night I wrote in my account book: Where do I stand? I think, instead, I'm still sitting on a fence. And this snake fence is growing most uncomfortable. What am I worth? Less than before I bailed out John McCowen.

CHAPTER 19

What Friends Can Do

Bringing the mutilated corpses to Philadelphia was as powerful as John hoped it would be. Everyone—Quakers, politicians, businessmen, craftsmen, even immigrants—was outraged and scared to death. Israel Pemberton seemed shaken to the core.

I sat at my little desk, waiting to be sent running, while he talked to his wife.

"Mary, I'm grateful thee didn't see them. It was horrible!" he told her.

"But, my dear, thee was so calm when thee came home that evening."

"Aye, calm on the surface, but I've not had a peaceful sleep since. Those poor, butchered bodies haunt me still. How can any living person treat another so brutally?" He paced the carpeted floor.

"Does thee think now that Indians are truly savages, as many say?" Mary asked.

He flung his arms wide in frustration. "No! I still believe there is the Light of God within each of his creatures. But any one, pushed to his limit by circumstances beyond his control, is capable of extreme cruelty. I'm appalled to realize how thin is the veneer of civilization."

"Civilization?" she asked. "Does thee consider Indians civilized?"

He stopped pacing. His scowl faded as he thought. "I have always believed they were civilized, in some ways more than we are. They have been generous and kind with our people here in Pennsylvania. In fact, their honesty in keeping treaties has exceeded our own, to our shame."

"Then how could they attack and kill settlers so?"

"That's exactly the question, Mary! What has cracked the veneer of civilization enough to make such noble men resort to brutish acts? What has gone wrong here in Pennsylvania, where we've lived peacefully together for so long?"

"It was hardly civilized of that young man from Easton to treat dead bodies so disrespectfully. They should have been tenderly washed and dressed for burial and mourned by their friends. Instead, he piled them onto a wagon and jounced them all the way down here. Then he threw them on the Assembly Hall steps and displayed them in all their gore. To me, that's nearly as shocking as the way they died." Mary shuddered at the thought.

My master took her gently in his arms, and she sobbed on his shoulder. "Thee mourns for them thyself, though thee knew none of them," he said.

She nodded.

"On both sides people react in less than human ways. Thus brutality breeds brutality. But what causes it? Could *I* be capable of such behavior?" He stepped away from her and began pacing again.

I was shocked to hear him say that, after what he had said to me earlier.

"I can't believe thee could!" Mary exclaimed. "Thee is full of the Light. Thee waits for the Spirit to lead thy ways."

"But, deep down, Mary, I know that if Indians, or anyone else, attacked thee as those settlers were attacked, I would want to kill every one of them."

"Thee would?" Mary gasped.

"Aye, I'd want to. I'd be that full of rage. But I hope I wouldn't act out my rage in that way. If I did, I'd be as bad as the murderers. I hope I'd leave vengeance to the Lord, or at least to the government. I *hope* I could restrain myself." But still he paced. I could see he doubted himself.

"Well, I pray thee never has occasion to find out!" Mary said as she left the room.

He kept on talking, but to himself, not to me, I think. "We never should have let things come to this. Our Founder would be ashamed of us. I'm ashamed of us, ashamed of myself. We haven't been vigilant enough. We assumed the government was handling relations with the Indians well enough. And look where our complacency has led! How could we have been so blind?"

Then I realized he was tormented by the same questions I was. He was blaming himself for the murders Indians were committing. Only my questions were about just one Indian and whatever he might do. My master was taking on responsibility for the whole province and all Indians. No wonder he was upset!

Reports of attacks on settlers poured in from the frontier, especially along the boundary of the Walking Purchase. Governor Morris kept asking the Assembly for a militia, and the Assembly kept throwing the matter back on his desk, insisting the Proprietors pay their fair share.

Every once in a while some Iroquois came to town, and the governor urged them to control the Delaware. In the past, the Iroquois had kept the Delaware in line, calling them a woman tribe and saying they couldn't make war without Iroquois permission. But now the Delaware were ignoring them.

The Iroquois could not understand why the government of Pennsylvania refused to take up arms directly against the French. Again and again the Iroquois offered to join us. They even warned that if we did not declare war against the French, the tribes would join the French against us. But the Assembly was locked in impasse.

Finally, near the end of the year, the legislature approved £50,000 "for the King's use." They knew that the money would be used for defense, but if they didn't say outright that it was for war, their consciences were somehow clear. It sure seemed like splitting hairs to me. And the Proprietors agreed to make a "gift," not a tax assessment, of £5,000. It had taken months and months to figure out the right words for the deal, months when lots of settlers were killed. Governor Morris sent Benjamin Franklin to Easton to decide where to build forts and to organize local militias.

Quakers were greatly upset with these preparations for war. We still hoped for a peaceful settlement with the Indians.

CHAPTER 20

The Light of God Within

By the end of Second Month, I was getting nervous. Each morning, I noticed the sun rising a minute or so earlier than the day before. Although I carried more messages each day, the sky was still light when I came home. Spring was coming. Pa would be checking his fields to decide when he could begin plowing. "Thee can work for Israel Pemberton for now, Noble, but thee must return for spring planting," he had said.

Planting, not plowing, I told myself. He wouldn't hold it against me if I stayed until halfway through Fourth Month.

I dreaded the thought of returning to the farm. I had saved every shilling I earned, except for John's bail, and I had a small sack of pennies from tips. I had bought a saw and a plane, and in my spare time I had built a toolbox with room for all the tools I hoped to acquire. But I still lacked most of what I needed.

In the homes where Pemberton sent me, I saw fine furniture of the kind I longed to make. I studied the lines and tried to figure out the construction while I waited for return messages. It was hard to keep my hands in my pockets and not run them over the gleaming waxed surfaces. It was hard to keep my mouth shut. I wanted to ask questions of my own besides getting answers for Friend Pemberton.

I really cared about what Friend Pemberton was trying to do. When I heard of Indians attacking settlers, when I thought of Broken Blade, I hoped I was a little part of the solution myself. Settlers and Indians wanted the same things. There must be a peaceable way out of this.

Besides, Pa's expectations weighed on my conscience. I hadn't really promised I'd come back, but Pa thought I had, and I knew he was expecting me. What would he do if I just didn't come? Would he take a day off and come to find me? Would he cause trouble for me with Friend Pemberton? Would he disown me and cut me out of the family?

All these possibilities felt dire, but leaving the city and returning to the farm seemed even worse.

By the middle of Third Month my master noticed my distress. One evening after I had delivered all the messages and responses, he said, "Sit down, Noble. I think thee is troubled. Tell me about it."

"I may have to leave soon, and I very much want to stay!" I exploded.

"What is this about?"

"Pa expects me to come home for spring planting, and it's time for that any day now."

"Did thee promise to return?"

"I don't think I made any promise, but he counts on me."

"And thee doesn't want to go back?"

"Nay. I haven't earned enough for all the tools I need. But besides that, I . . . I . . ." I hesitated, not knowing how to explain.

"What?"

"Well, I know what I do counts for very little, and thee could easily replace me with a lad from the Almshouse, like Tom. But I want to see thy efforts for peace succeed. I have a personal reason for needing these attacks to end."

"Oh?"

I took a deep breath. I had told no one but Christopher and Jedediah that I had freed Broken Blade.

"On the way home from Wills's Creek last summer, when John McCowen sent me up the mountain to retrieve his pelts, I freed an Indian pinned behind a fallen tree. Ever since, I've worried that he might be attacking settlers and that their blood is on my hands. But I couldn't just leave him there to die."

Pemberton leaned forward intently. "Why could thee not leave him there to die?"

"I considered it. I had a real argument with myself. But in the end, I just couldn't walk away from someone suffering. We were helping John. How could I not help this other person?"

"Aha! Noble, that was the Light of God directing thee that day."

"Aye, I thought so at the time, but what if I saved his life only for him to kill settlers? Am I responsible for their deaths? That's why it's so important to me to help in even my small way to bring about peace." In distress, I was wringing my hands and popping my knuckles.

"If the Light directed thee that day on the mountainside, then I trust that thee did the right thing. That Indian may be involved in these attacks, or not. We have no way of knowing. But thee did the right thing. And no, I don't believe anyone's blood is on thy hands."

I breathed out in relief.

"Thee has been a faithful servant to me, Noble. I'm convinced God sent thee when I needed a runner. Thee has quickly learned thy way around the city, but, more than that, thy interest in achieving peace has made my work easier. I wouldn't be surprised if thee has entered into conversation with my correspondents to clarify my written words. Thee is helpful in bringing me oral responses because thee understands the issues involved. Aye, I *could* find another lad at the Almshouse, but I doubt I could find one as intelligent, committed, and faithful as thee has proved to be. I should be very sorry to see thee leave."

"But I can feel Pa closing in on me. He expects his sons to farm with him. He planned for each of us to have a different trade on the side. Mine was meant to be woodworking. But that's not the way I want to live. I want to make fine furniture and live in the city where I can help make the world a better place, or at least my corner of it."

"Has thee told him what thee hopes to do?"

"Aye. He thinks it's another of my hare-brained ideas."

Pemberton smiled and shook his head. Then he said, "Noble, thee followed the Light that day on the mountainside. Now thee must listen again, and when the way becomes clear, thee must follow that urging. Thee was brave enough to free a trapped Indian. Now be brave enough to tell thy father thee must live thy own life."

Thee doesn't know Pa, I thought.

CHAPTER 21

The Past Revealed

Early in Fourth Month, Governor Morris declared war on the Delaware and offered bounties for scalps.

Israel Pemberton was horrified when he read the news in The *Pennsylvania Gazette*. "Listen to this, Mary," he exclaimed to his wife.

> "For every male Indian prisoner above twelve years old that shall be delivered at any of the government's forts or towns, $150; for every female Indian prisoner or male prisoner of twelve years old and under, delivered as above, $130; for the scalp of every male Indian of above twelve years old, $130; for the scalp of every Indian woman, $50."

"Oh, no!" Mary cried. "No Indian will be safe anywhere in the entire colony."

My master smacked the folded newspaper against his palm. "William Penn would turn over in his grave to hear this news! He intended us to live in peace and harmony with the Indians. But here's a governor appointed by his sons promising rewards for Indian scalps! Friends must *do* something about it. *I* must do something!"

"What can thee do, Israel? Thee is no longer in the Assembly, and Governor Morris is not one to listen to thy advice."

He paced faster and faster. "True enough, he'll not listen to me. I don't know what advice I could even offer at this point. Why have relationships with our Indian friends gone so wrong? For seventy years we've lived peacefully together. What could have upset them so much that they would strike settlers?"

The same old questions.

I waited in the corner of the study, running my finger and thumb around and around the rim of my tricorn hat. Then I remembered Christopher's story around the campfire on the way to Wills's Creek.

"Does thee know of the Walking Purchase?" I asked my master.

"Oh, yes. I recall when it happened, nigh twenty years ago now," he replied.

He explained to Mary, "The Proprietors claimed they had found a deed dated 1688. Supposedly it gave them land from the Delaware River 'as far as a man could walk in a day and a half' and from there back to the river. The Proprietors decided to claim that land, in 1737, I believe it was. The Indians didn't recall the deed or anything of the transaction, and this was their prime settled land. But they agreed to honor it. Is that what thee refers to, Noble?"

"Aye, that's it."

"How does thee know of it? Thee is too young to remember it."

"I heard about it from Christopher, our scout on the trip to Wills's Creek. The way he told it, the Proprietors' men advertised for the fastest runners and offered to pay them according to how far they could run. Then they even blazed and cleared the trail for them. On the day of the survey, the Indians started out walking with the men, but when they broke into a run, the Indians called out, 'Walk, not run!' The runners ignored them, so the Indians finally gave up in disgust. The runners went about twice as far as the Indians expected. And then, instead of drawing the line due east back to the Delaware River, they angled northeast, so they staked out about two and a half times what the Indians thought they were giving up."

"How dishonest!" Mary exclaimed. "No wonder they are upset! But if that was twenty years ago . . ."

"Aye, they appealed," Pemberton replied, "and as far as I know, the Crown is still supposed to be looking into it. Does thee believe, Noble, that the Walking Purchase is the cause of all these attacks?"

"Christopher thought it might be one cause."

"Mayhap our Proprietors and their governors have been dishonest with the Indians in more than one land dealing. If we could only hear from the Delaware just what their complaints are . . ." Turning to me, Pemberton asked, half jokingly, "Does thee know any Indians, Noble? Thee is always surprising me."

I ducked my head sheepishly, "Nay. I see them here in the city from time to time, but I don't speak their language."

"And where is thy friend Christopher?"

"He said he would be staying in Philadelphia looking for work as an interpreter, either with the government or traders. But I have not seen him."

"Don't Indians sometimes come to the city to meet with the Assembly? Would thy brother James know?" Mary wondered.

"He would certainly know when a delegation arrives," Pemberton replied. "And Friends within the Assembly might investigate the Proprietors' dealings with the Indians. I still believe that if we could find out what has angered them, we could redress their grievances and bring about a peaceful solution. That's it! That's what Friends can do!"

Turning to me, he said, "I won't take time to write all this. Run to James and urge him to come over so we can make a plan. If he can't come just now, tell him the gist of our conversation so he will begin thinking of ways to help."

In the weeks that followed, I wore a path between our house and the Assembly Hall. Friends in the Assembly asked the governor for all documents dealing with land purchases from Indian tribes. He refused. He said the Assembly was overstepping its bounds in requesting them. But Friends kept at it, examining land records and meeting often to check their findings. Every day I met other runners as we criss-crossed the city.

Gradually a pattern emerged. It was clear that the Proprietors had unfairly claimed thousands of acres and then sold huge plantations to their wealthy friends, who in turn sold off smaller parcels at great profit to themselves. In each transaction, Indians were forced off their traditional lands and pushed farther west.

None of these deals was as obvious as the Walking Purchase, but added together, I could see why the tribes were boiling over. Indians believed a deal was a deal, and our government had betrayed them again and again. And with the British army far away in New York, there was no one to stop them. The only hope seemed to be with Quakers who could remind the Delaware of their original pact with William Penn.

Israel Pemberton waited for a chance to meet some Indians in Philadelphia. And I watched to see how he furthered his plans for peace while the government worked in the opposite direction.

He was like Pa in some ways. Both knew how to get things done. But instead of driving horses, Friend Pemberton drove politics. Instead of planting crops, he planted ideas. Instead of lending money to earn more, he spent money to make good things happen. Both he and Pa were fair in their dealings, but I could see how other people might think both of them high handed. Mayhap I'd learned enough from Pa, but I still had plenty to learn from Friend Pemberton.

As I found out how often Indians had been cheated, I realized how foolish I had been when I set out for Wills's Creek with the wagon train. I had thought the British Army could teach those Indians a lesson. I hadn't even considered how they might do it. Of course the army planned to wipe out Indians the way Indians were trying to wipe out settlers. How stupid of me!

I had new understandings of words like *savage* and *heathen*. I even thought of *civilized* in a new way. And *responsible*, too. How many times had I asked myself whether I was responsible for murders Broken Blade might commit? Instead of stewing about guilt, wouldn't it be more responsible to try to right the wrongs that were causing the murders? Wasn't that what Pemberton was trying to do?

When I finally stopped beating myself up with guilt about my own stupidity, I was grateful all over again for my job as runner. In a small way, I was working for peace myself. In fact, even wanting tools was taking second place to wanting these peace efforts to succeed.

CHAPTER 22

The Future Unfolds

In the middle of Fourth Month, James Pemberton told his brother and sister-in-law, "A delegation from the Six Nations of the Iroquois is coming to Philadelphia. Would thee like to meet with them, Israel?"

Mary interrupted, "Isn't it the Delaware, not the Iroquois, with whom we want peace?"

"That's right, Mary," James replied, "but the Iroquois handle matters for the Delaware, and the Iroquois are still friendly, or at least neutral, with the English. What does thee think, Israel?"

"Let's have a dinner for them after they've finished their business with the governor. We'll invite some of the leading Friends, too, and have a conversation about the Delaware. Will thee extend the invitation, James? Mary, can thee handle the arrangements for the dinner?"

Mary hesitated. "Indians here, in our home?"

"Aye, Mary. It's the Friendly thing to do, doesn't thee think? Hospitality. Though these Iroquois are strangers to us, we are bound by William Penn's treaty to deal with them as brothers. This could be the opening for peace. Thee will see," he promised.

Right away, my master sent me with a message to Governor Morris because he did not want to act behind the government's back. The governor agreed to let the

Pembertons hold their dinner on the condition that Conrad Weiser, Pennsylvania's agent for Indian Affairs, attend and report back to him.

By now I had delivered messages not only to the governor but also to Benjamin Franklin, Conrad Weiser, and many other rich and famous people in Philadelphia. I knew my way around, and I knew who was who. But the very idea of Indians coming to the Pemberton house for dinner made my palms sweat and my breath come fast. Indians! In our house! What if . . . ? What if, after they ate Gwyneth's company dinner, they rose up and murdered us all?

How I dreaded the thought of delivering invitations to the Indians! Even though I told myself Indians were not savages, I could still picture those murdered settlers on the way to Wills's Creek. I could still feel the hatred in Broken Blade's eyes as I worked to free him. I wasn't sure I could go up to an Indian and hand him an invitation to come to our house.

Instead, James Pemberton took care of invitations at the Assembly Hall, where the Indians were meeting with the delegates. The Iroquois accepted. Then my master sent me around the city to invite leading Quakers.

Although Conrad Weiser would serve as one interpreter, we needed a few more. I mentioned Christopher to my master.

"He sounds quite capable, Noble. Does thee know where he lives?"

"Nay, but I can try to find him."

"Very well. Go to the Assembly Hall and see if anyone knows him. Or mayhap Benjamin Franklin would know. Thee might check with him."

I went first to Franklin's printing shop on High Street. It was next to the post office, and those two locations were among the busiest in the city. If Christopher were still in Philadelphia, someone there would surely know how to find him.

Someone did. "I remember him. Check next door at the Indian Queen Tavern. I believe he stays there."

"Thank thee, Friend," I said and hurried next door.

It took a while for my eyes to adjust to the dim light inside the tavern. Men of all kinds filled the Windsor chairs around oak tables. The air was thick with tobacco smoke and political talk. In the back corner I saw Christopher at the same time he noticed me.

"Hullo, young Friend," Christopher called. "What brings you here?

"Hullo, Christopher. Could I speak to thee outdoors, please?"

He excused himself from his friends and followed me out to the street. I led him to the swampy area by Dock Creek, away from anyone who might overhear what I had to say. Briefly, I explained how I had come to work for Israel Pemberton, how distressed Pemberton was about the government's treatment of the Delaware, and how he needed an interpreter to help with the dinner for the Iroquois.

Christopher frowned. "Noble, does Pemberton realize he is interfering with the government? We're at war with the Delaware!"

"Aye, he knows that very well. But it's not the Delaware he's entertaining. It's the Iroquois. He wants them to help him achieve peace with the Delaware. Besides, he has the governor's permission."

"The governor knows what he's up to?"

"The governor said he could conduct the dinner on two conditions: Conrad Weiser had to attend, and the governor wants minutes of their discussion."

"I see. Weiser would be the interpreter, then, wouldn't he? Why am I needed?"

"Because it is a long table, and one interpreter couldn't keep up with all the conversations."

"All right, then, I'll come. I never could turn down a dinner. But I hope Pemberton is not making a mistake."

"I hope so, too! Thank thee, Christopher. See thee tomorrow at Pembertons'!"

On the nineteenth day of Fourth Month, Israel and Mary Pemberton hosted a mid-day dinner for the Iroquois. Six Indians came, along with seven Quakers (counting the three Pembertons) and four interpreters. The Iroquois and interpreters gathered outside our gate for their grand entrance, while the Quakers inside peeked out the windows. Ralph waited at the door to let them in.

It was scary to see that many Indians together and know that they were coming into our house. There were four men, a woman, and a little boy. The men were dressed in a strange combination of English and Indian clothes, but even though they tried to look like proper Englishmen, no one would ever mistake them. Their shaved heads, dangling earrings, and small leather pouches hanging from leather strips around their necks gave them away. The woman wore a skirt of woven cloth and a deerskin shirt decorated with shells and beads. The little boy had on only a breechcloth. Mary Pemberton swallowed hard when she saw them.

The Iroquois had no weapons with them, though, and the interpreters joked and laughed with them outside. Three of the interpreters were English. The other was part-Indian Andrew Montour. Finally Conrad Weiser knocked at the front door, Ralph opened it and welcomed everyone, and they all filed in. Christopher winked at me as he entered the dining room. That made me feel a little easier.

During the dinner, I waited in the hall, ready as always to carry messages. I could hear a pleasant hum of voices and soft clinks of silver and crystal but understood nothing of the conversation.

Then I heard the table being cleared and chairs scooted back. The serious part of the gathering was about to begin. I inched closer to the door. With only one person speaking at a time, mayhap I could hear what was being said. How I hoped this meeting would lead to peace with the Delaware!

My master stood and spoke first. "Brethren, I am glad to see you here, and to have an opportunity of informing you that as William Penn and our fathers who first settled this province were men of peace, against all wars, so there are still many of us their children who hold the same principles, and we hope there are many of your people who still have a love and regard for their old friends."

I could hear him sit down, and then another chair scraped backwards. I peeped in the keyhole. Andrew Montour stood to translate Pemberton's words. Then the old, dignified Indian leader, Scarouady, responded. When he finished speaking, Christopher stood to translate what he had said:

"I am very glad to hear this account; we love that principle of peace, and wish all mankind were of the same mind, knowing it would prevent any cause of difference or contention between us and the English, and take away the occasion of war."

Just as I tuned my ears to the strange dignity of these speeches, someone pounded the door knocker outside. I backed away from the dining room door and nearly bumped into Ralph as he came flying to answer. Neither of us wanted the conference disturbed. Ralph flung open the front door.

I gasped. There was Pa, his hand still raised to knock again.

Ralph said, "How may I help thee?"

"I've come for my son. There he is, behind thee in the hallway."

Surprised, Ralph turned to me. I knew there was no look of welcome on my face.

I had to get Pa out of there! I didn't want him to interrupt Friend Pemberton's meeting by yelling at me.

"Hullo, Pa." I ran to the door, grabbed Pa's elbow and turned him around. "Look, Pa, something really important is happening right now. Let's go to the garden to talk." Before he could say a word, I steered him to the gazebo, out of earshot from the house.

My stomach churned. Why did Pa have to come today, right in the middle of the dinner for peace? I couldn't leave now! I couldn't! But I was sure Pa would insist.

If I went back now, for the rest of my life I'd be at Pa's beck and call, Pa's ideas of when to plant and harvest, Pa's ideas of when to buy and sell. I'd lose all my woodworking skills. I'd pound a nail from time to time and saw an odd board, but mostly I'd be Pa's servant. He'd use my strength and labor and pay me with promises. I had to stand up for myself.

As our footsteps crunched the fine gravel of the garden path, I had another shock. I could see the top of Pa's head! I had never seen that small bald spot before. I must have grown! I was bigger than Pa! Confidence surged through me. I could do this. I had become a man!

Once in the gazebo, Pa turned with a grim, no-nonsense look to face me. "'Tis time for spring planting, Noble. I expected thee home by now."

"I'm not coming home, Pa," I replied quietly.

"Was that not our agreement? Didn't thee promise?" Pa's voice was like cold iron.

"That was thy understanding. I think I did not promise. I didn't mean to mislead thee, Pa, but I cannot leave now." I still spoke softly, hoping Pa wouldn't yell at me.

A red glint came into Pa's eyes and he grew louder. "I think thee *did* promise. That was why I allowed thee to leave during harvest. Has thee forgotten all thee knows about farming? Timing is crucial!"

I took a deep breath and made my low voice intense. "Aye, timing *is* crucial, for thee and for me. And I must stay here. If I leave now, my life will never be my own. I'll always be thy son, but I don't want to be under thy thumb."

Pa snapped, "I never should have let thee go to Wills's Creek with Enoch! He's poisoned thy mind. Just because he was fool enough to reject my offer doesn't mean thee should do the same."

I was astonished. "Pa, Enoch said virtually nothing

to me on the whole trip! Only once, when we sold John's pelts, did he even mention thy plan. This has nothing to do with Enoch."

Pa stared at me. I could see wheels going around in his head. "Thee has grown citified," he accused. "Israel Pemberton has tainted thee with promises of his own."

"Nay, Pa. The truth is, I've found the Light and must follow God's leading. I'm on a path of my own, and I'd be wrong to give it up." I spoke as if I really meant it, but I was trembly inside.

"The Light? God's leading? Sounds more like stubborn willfulness to me." Pa's voice dripped with scorn.

"I've thought and prayed, Pa, and the way has become clear. I do believe it is the Light of God."

Pa stamped his foot and turned away. After a short silence, he said, "Be sensible, son. If thee farms with me and thy brothers, thee will have financial security and after my death a farm of thy own."

"Thee doesn't understand. I don't want a farm of my own. I choose to be a cabinetmaker."

"How can thee make a living as a cabinetmaker? Thee has worked here six months. How many tools has thee bought? At home we have everything we need to make a decent income for all of us by working together."

"I have saved every penny I've earned and bought tools as I can afford them. I've learned so much about furniture, designs, craftsmanship, and all I've learned has only made me want to know more. If I go home with thee, my dreams will die."

"What is thy worth by now? Where does thee stand? Has thee used the account book I gave thee?"

I knew he wanted a clear answer in pounds and

shillings. But these were the questions that haunted me. How many evenings as I wrote in the account book did I ask myself where I stood, on questions of what it means to be a man, what it means to be a Quaker, on questions of peace and violence, on fair dealings, on guilt for freeing Broken Blade? Back to the snake fence.

What was my worth? To whom? To Friend Pemberton, I was a trusted servant. To John McCowen I was a friend in need. To Broken Blade, I was a rescuer. But if I didn't stand up for myself right now, I'd be worth nothing as Pa's little boy.

"Aye, Pa, I've used the account book. And where I stand, where I must stand, is on my own two feet, or I won't be worth much in my own opinion."

A distant look settled on his face, a look I'd never seen. Then he said, "If thee makes this choice, thee turns thy back on our family, Noble. Thee will always be welcome in our home, but thee cuts thyself off from working together to build a fine farm and a good life for all of us. Is thee ready to choose that?"

"Aye, Pa. I'm sorry to disappoint thee, but I'm quite sure."

Pa shook his head. Defeat and disgust lined his face.

He said, "We'll see whether this is another one of thy hare-brained ideas or truly God's Light leading you."

"I need to go back inside now, Pa. I'm on duty."

"What's going on in there so important that thee hurried me out here?"

"Pembertons are having a dinner for Indians to talk about peace."

"That'll be the day," he said.

I wanted so much to tell him about how important it

was, but he wasn't ready to listen. And I really did need to get back to work.

Pa jammed his fists into his pockets and started to go. Then he turned back. "Thee looks taller, Noble." And he left.

Watching Pa mount his horse, I felt a surge of confidence and elation I had never known. I basked in it till he rounded the corner, and then, head held high, I marched back to Pemberton's house.

The Iroquois were shaking hands with the Quakers on their way out the front door as I came in the back. Conrad Weiser was saying to Pemberton, "One more thing: you need wampum next time. They won't be much impressed unless you give them at least a few strings of wampum. A belt would be even better."

"Do you mean we should *bribe* them? With beads?"

"Oh, no. The tribes use wampum to emphasize the importance of speeches and decisions. A single string of beads might be given for each main point of a speech. A belt is given for a whole treaty. The longer the string or belt, the more important it is. White beads signify peace, black means war. Without wampum, your words lack not only importance but also authority."

"I see. Yes, of course. But where does one get strings and belts of wampum?"

"There are Indian women here in the city who could make some for you. Be generous if you want to make a favorable impression."

"Would you arrange that for me? Here is some money." He shook a handful of coins out of his money pouch. "Will this be enough?"

Weiser smiled broadly. "This will impress them, I'm sure. I'll take care of it."

As the door closed behind Weiser, Pemberton turned to me with a great smile of satisfaction. "That went very well, I thought. We'll meet again in two days, so thee will have many errands to run. By the way, what was that pounding at the door?"

"That was Pa, come to fetch me back to the farm."

"And?"

"I told him I must live my own life."

"And?"

"We argued a while, but I stood firm. I told him I would follow God's leading."

"And then?"

"He thinks I'm making a mistake, but he left without me."

"Hmmm. I see. Well done, Noble. By the way, thee looks a little taller."

CHAPTER 23

Preparations for Peace

Two days later, the same six Indians came back, bringing along eight or ten others. There were more Quakers, too. The drawing room was filled. Tom and I pressed our ears to the closed door and took turns peeking through the keyhole.

Conrad Weiser had brought an impressive supply of wampum, so as the meeting began, Friend Pemberton gave Scarouady the first string of white beads and said, "Brethren: We are glad to find you retain so lively and affectionate a remembrance of William Penn and our forefathers and the friendship that subsisted between them and your fathers. We have long lain hid and almost buried by the great numbers of other people who are come into this province. Many of them have different principles from us; yet there is a great number in this city, in other parts of the province, and some on the frontiers who share these same peaceable principles, and who love you as our brethren.

"We are sorrowful that differences have arisen between your cousins the Delaware and our people. We want to work to restore peace, and if they will stop doing further mischief, we are ready to stand between them and the government, that they may be forgiven. As a proof of our sincerity, we give you this belt, which you see is white, without any mixture, as our love and friendship to you is."

Pemberton held up a large belt of wampum and then continued, "It is made of many small pieces of little weight or strength before they were knit together, but now it is strong and firm. So we, when collected and united together, shall appear to our brethren. With this belt we desire you to let both the Six Nations and the Delaware know that we have not forgotten the love and kindness of their fathers to ours. As men of the same peaceable principle, we are ready to help in any manner we can to stop the present bloodshed and pave the way for a treaty. Then all uneasiness may be freely discussed. When we know the grounds of their discontent, we will work to remove them in every respect."

He turned to Christopher, who translated for him. Then he handed over the large belt of white wampum.

Scarouady stood to accept it. He showed it around to the others, who nodded in admiration. Then he replied in his Indian language. When he finished, Andrew Montour put his speech into English. "Brethren, we are glad to hear what you have said. By this belt we understand that you offer to stand up as William Penn's children and that the old principles of peace and love are yet in being. Your fathers declared that they had nothing but love and good will in their hearts to all men. We thought people like that were all dead and buried in the bushes or ashes. We are very glad that there are some of the same men living and that you offer to mediate between our cousins the Delaware and this government. This misfortune came upon us as if an evil spirit had arisen from under the ground and spread all over the country, and blood was spilt before we had time to think. But we must now all apply to the good Spirit, to assist both you and us to subdue the evil Spirit."

The Quakers seemed fascinated by the old Indian's beautiful words. Pemberton replied, "Brethren, as you are wise men, we ask you to think how we may put a stop to the bloodshed. Many of our friends, who hold these same peaceable principles, live in different parts of the province and some on the very frontiers. If something is not done soon, they may be destroyed, among others. Therefore we want to put a speedy stop to the shedding of blood." Then, instead of another string of wampum, Pemberton gave a string of medals with the King's head engraved on them.

Scarouady answered, "Brethren, we will think of the best way to advise you, and we will convey our thoughts before we leave town. We shall fix the medals you gave us on our breasts, and whenever we look on them, we shall remember, and let others know, that some of William Penn's descendants, of the same principles, are living."

At that, the Indians rose, shook hands with the Quakers, and took their leave.

In the hallway, I waited.

Again, Conrad Weiser stayed behind to speak to Pemberton.

"What will happen next?" Pemberton asked.

"They will talk among themselves for a day or two. Then they will want another meeting to give you their considered advice before they return to their home in Onondaga."

"Will we need more wampum?"

"No, it's their turn now to present you with wampum. You'll see."

"Thank you, Colonel Weiser, for guiding us through this. Thee does far more than translate words!"

"I want peace as much as you do. You realize you are putting yourselves at great risk when you offer to stand between the Delaware and your own government, don't you? After all, Pennsylvania has declared war on the Delaware. You could be considered to be aiding the enemy."

"Governor Morris may well send word to the Proprietors in England that we are traitors. But it takes months for letters to pass from here to London and back, and we Quakers still dominate the Assembly here. We *are* risking our fortunes and our very lives, but we hope to achieve peace before the Proprietors can have our heads. If we don't try, we may all lose our heads to the Indians before the Proprietors can act. But we are dealing with Iroquois, not Delaware, and so far the Iroquois are still friends of our government, so this can't be treason."

An even larger number of Iroquois and one Delaware came to Pemberton's house two days later. This time several of their women came, too. The same twenty Quakers showed up. Again, Tom and I listened at the doorway.

After the usual polite preliminaries, Scarouady presented strings of white wampum and gestured to three of his companions, "We shall send these three Indians to the Delaware tribes to let our cousins know there are a people risen in Philadelphia who desire to have peace restored. They will tell them they must cease from doing any more mischief and not be afraid. They must be willing to treat with you. Perhaps it may please the Most High to bring them back in safety with an agreeable answer. If they come back, take notice of them as of your firm friends. We want very much that through your efforts the former treaties of friendship between us may now be renewed. May the chain of friendship be kept bright and never rust again!"

Pemberton thanked him and gave gifts of flowered silk handkerchiefs to all the Indians. Again, everyone shook hands, and the conferences ended. On his way out, Christopher whispered to me, "Now you *will* be busy, I warrant!"

Christopher was right! Pemberton sent a flurry of letters to members of the Pennsylvania Assembly, to Conrad Weiser, and to Sir William Johnson, who was in charge of all Indian affairs in the North American colonies. All these letters explained the Quakers' commitment to peace with the Delaware.

It was the end of Fifth Month before the three Indians who carried the message to the Delaware came safely back to Philadelphia. Governor Morris announced a peace conference to be held in Easton the end of July.

"Why Easton?" I asked Friend Pemberton. "It's scarcely a village, John told me."

"Why, indeed! The only reason I can think of is that the Proprietors own land up there and want their Philadelphia friends to buy it from them."

When the Assembly voted £300 for conference expenses, Pemberton snorted in disgust. "That won't be nearly enough to cover gifts for the Indians. Quakers will have to make up the difference."

He sent me to gather wealthy Friends for a meeting. "Governor Morris will spend most of that £300 on his own color guard," Pemberton told them. "We need to raise funds ourselves for gifts for the Delaware. If we are to succeed in waging peace, we should accumulate several wagonloads of presents."

Before the evening ended, these wealthy Friends had pledged over £2000 of their own money for the cause. That would buy plenty of gifts for the Indians. After that, my errands took me more frequently to the docks and warehouses than to the Assembly Hall, and I returned with pledges of wagons and all sorts of supplies. It looked as if I might be going on another wagon train trip, a trip of a very different kind. Instead of bringing General Braddock supplies for war, we'd be bringing Indians gifts for peace.

One evening as I trudged up the narrow stairs to my third floor room, I ran my hand over the smoothly shaped banister and realized how little I had thought lately about my own future. Woodworking could wait. Peace must come first, or I might not live to become a cabinetmaker.

Then one day Pemberton sent me to William Savery for his pledge of support. Even before I found the exact address, I could hear the drone of a great wheel lathe and smell wood and glue. Friend Savery was a cabinetmaker! I entered the shop, scuffling through curls of shavings on the floor, and stopped in my tracks to watch him chiseling a design on a spindle turned by the lathe. Unaware that I was there, he stopped to measure his work with a pair of calipers. The apprentice turning the lathe coughed to alert his master that someone had entered the shop.

Friend Savery turned and asked, "How may I help thee?"

Oh! How I would like to be helping *thee*! I thought. But I only said, "I've come from Friend Pemberton to ask thy support for the peace efforts with the Delaware."

"Aye, I have been expecting thee. My pledge is in that envelope over there. I wish I could do more, but that is all I can manage right now. 'Tis good of Israel to take on this project."

I was silent, my hands tingling at the sight of fine wood and tools aplenty. Savery noticed my look of longing and asked, "Is there anything else?"

I came to myself with a start. "Does thee think to hire any help? I have finished my apprenticeship with Friend Williamson of Chester County, but I have not been able to find work without tools of my own. That's why I am now a runner, to save money for tools."

"I see. Well, young Friend, at present I have all the workers I need, but perhaps in six months or so, I could use thy help. Will thee have tools by then?"

"I hope to. I have one plane, a saw, and a brace with two bits so far. I am paid a shilling a week, and I save money from tips as well."

"Thee may earn some extra on the way to Easton. Thee will need saws, a miter box, and chisels. Perhaps I can find some work for thee in a few months."

I just nodded. I looked around the shop and saw three cabinetmakers, each working at his own bench well-stocked with his own tools. How I envied them!

That night, I drew my toolbox out from under my bed. The box itself was proof of my skill. The dove-tailed corners, the smooth joints, the clever holders for tools I had yet to buy, all bespoke my love of woodworking. But the box was nearly empty. How many tools could I acquire in six months? And when would John McCowen ever be able to repay me?

CHAPTER 24

Easton

At last we left for Easton. The Indians had been there a couple of weeks, waiting for Governor Morris. He had delayed so long that Friend Pemberton was worried the Indians might change their minds. It was hot in Philadelphia, hot and muggy. Sensible people who could afford it had already headed for the country. Our fine shirts stuck to our backs. I thought people who wore wigs in this weather were crazy, but there were many who wouldn't stick their heads out of doors without one.

The governor was one of them. When he left for Easton with his secretary, several Assemblymen, and a color guard from the British army, besides all their servants, they made quite a parade. I wondered how fancy they would look after a day on the road.

We left the day after the governor, about thirty of the weighty Quakers and their servants with wagonloads of gifts for the Indians. I got to drive one of the wagons, just behind Friend Pemberton on his fine horse. There was no wagon master or scout, no packhorses. And there were no women and children walking behind. In fact, the Quakers didn't even try to stay together.

As we drove north out of Philadelphia, we passed one elegant plantation after another, all belonging to wealthy Friends. These were country homes where they came to escape city heat and fever during summer months. Friend Pemberton had grown up in one of them, called Bolton. We stopped there for dinner.

Nothing on the trip to Wills's Creek compared to this! Instead of a tavern, this was almost a palace. Servants fed even wagoners like me on tables with cloths and china plates. We had a leisurely dinner and then set out again, stopping for afternoon tea at another Friend's home. And we spent the night at yet another grand estate. No sleeping under the wagon on this trip! Even I had a real bed.

The second day, the road was still wide and well traveled as we passed cultivated fields and orchards. But the farther north we went, the farther apart these plantations were.

I began to hear woodsmen's axes ringing through the forest, so many axes that it sounded like music, almost. Then we could hear shouts and a large tree falling. After only a brief pause, the axes rang out again. The forest grew thinner and thinner. We saw huge areas cleared, like the approach to Fort Cumberland. Was there a fort here? Then Friend Pemberton explained to me about the Durham Forge.

"They cut trees to make charcoal for the forge," he said. "They cut several acres a day to keep the furnace going, smelting pig iron to send to England."

As we passed the forge, he pointed out the pole building where the furnaces were and the mound where wood was slowly turned into charcoal by slow burning under all that dirt. Woodcutters' cottages surrounded the owner's great house.

At Durham, I could see docks along the river. Men

were loading long, low boats with chunks of iron to be poled down to Philadelphia. Then it would be transferred to ships bound for Bristol or Southampton in England. Other boats, with sails, were coming upriver against the swift current. I was surprised to see traffic on the river. On the way out to Wills's Creek we had seen only an occasional canoe, but here the river was as busy as a city street.

I tried to concentrate on what I was seeing so I wouldn't be thinking about Molly. It was hard to picture her married to Peter. He was so quiet and steady. She was . . . like quicksilver. Unpredictable, slippery, changeable . . . exciting. Had marriage settled her? And by now she must have had her baby. Would motherhood sit well upon her? Or would she still be able to send me into a tizzy? She always made me feel as if I had two left feet. And a knot in my tongue. Well, I guessed I'd find out. Surely I'd see them sometime during the peace conference.

I hoped to see John McCowen as well, and mayhap meet his family. I had heard nothing from him since his trip to Philadelphia. Would he repay my money?

Late afternoon on the second day, we could see Easton tucked in the point where the Lehigh River empties into the Delaware. It was tiny, no bigger than Wright's Ferry. Even though several ferry boats were crossing the Lehigh, we had to wait our turn. Across the river we could see bustle and commotion. There were more people there for the peace conference than people who lived in Easton! The locals were overwhelmed with this crowd on their doorsteps.

Friend Pemberton asked Vernon, the ferryman, what was the best inn in town, and Vernon said, "Mine, of course, but we're chock-a-block full. Same with all of 'em. Ye'll not find a bed tonight."

My master merely smiled and said nothing. I wondered if he would have to sleep on the blankets we were bringing to give the Indians.

He rode up to Bachmann's Tavern, the one that looked a little better than the rest, and went in. I waited outside with his horse and the wagon. After a few minutes he came out and said, "I'll be staying here, Noble. Find a place for the wagon, mayhap outside of town. I don't want these gifts to be seen until we are ready to distribute them. I want thee at hand in Easton, though. Find a place nearby to camp, learn who is staying where, and then be ready to carry my messages."

How had he managed to get a room? Did he buy out someone?

I said, "I have friends nearby on a farm. Mayhap they can hide the wagon."

"Fine," he said. "Come to me here after breakfast."

In the tavern I asked directions to Peter's farm and then inched the wagon through the milling crowd until I was in open country again. Before long, I was knocking on the door of the farmhouse. Peter came out to greet me. I didn't see Molly.

"Hullo, Peter."

"Noble! What a surprise! What brings you here?"

"I've been working as a runner for Friend Pemberton since I saw thee last. He leads the Quaker delegation supporting the Indians in the peace conference," I explained. "We brought a wagonload of gifts for the Indians and want to keep them hidden until time to present them. Could thee hide the wagon for us?"

Peter shook his head doubtfully. "I did say that if you ever came to Easton, you had a place to stay. But things are different now."

"Oh, I don't want to stay. I'm only looking for a safe place to hide the wagon."

"You must know that people around here don't think much of Quakers."

"All Quakers, or just the Assemblymen?"

"Assemblymen, for sure, but any Quaker is unpopular right now. People blame all of 'em for not letting us defend ourselves against the Indians."

"We do care about settlers' being attacked. We just have a different way of solving the problem."

"You're not working against the government, are you? Now that they're finally doing something about these heathen attacks, we don't want anything to go wrong."

Suddenly Molly was at Peter's elbow. She must have been listening on the other side of the door. Without so much as a "Good day," she said, "Noble, ye're still me friend and always will be, but we've had so much trouble with them savages up here. We've little Sarah to look after," she said, snuggling her baby.

I stared at her. She was grown up, no longer the girl who had asked for my friendship. Now, instead of inviting me to play, she was thinking of consequences. I took a deep breath and tried to respect this new woman.

"Molly's right," Peter said. "First the Assembly refused even to let us defend ourselves. Finally they let us form a militia, with officers, weapons, ammunition, and pay, even. But then they called a truce before there was even a battle. Now they've brought all these redskins here, where people are scared to death of them."

"And with good reason!" Molly said. "Even as little Sarah was comin' into the world, bloody savages were attackin' the farm next to ours. I've never been so scared in me life! What kind of welcome is that for a babe newly born?"

Peter went on, "So tell us how Pemberton and his Quaker friends are supporting the Indians but not working against the government."

"We're working for *peace*. People can only trust each other when everyone gets a fair deal. Remember Christopher told us last summer that our government has been cheating the Delaware in land purchases? They don't trust us anymore. Friends are here to make sure they are treated fairly. We should have been doing that all along, but we trusted the government more than they deserved."

"Ah!" Molly's eyes brightened. "So yer actually working *for* the government by keepin' 'em honest, *makin'* 'em deal fairly."

"That's right. If we hold the government's feet to the fire, so to speak, finally the Delaware will trust us. Then they will let us all live peacefully."

"How will you do that?" Peter asked.

"We want to make sure that the Delaware have their own interpreters, so they understand what they are agreeing to. And we've brought gifts for the Delaware because the Assembly didn't offer enough to be convincing. If the government is generous, tribes feel respected. And just by being *with* them, we're showing good will."

"Good will to the redskins," Peter said, "but I imagine the government thinks you are interfering."

"Aye, they do. And I suppose we really are. But if we can get them to behave honorably, we can expect tribes to respond in kind. So we think we're working for the government."

"*Quakers* can expect redskins to respond in kind." Peter corrected me. "The rest of us aren't at all sure of that. I joined the militia in December, along with most of the men around here. We've seen these heathens. They're barbarians."

"But Peter," I pleaded, "until recently they were friendly enough."

"I hope you're right. In any case, you are welcome to leave the wagon here. Just don't bring any of your redskin friends around our farm."

Terror flashed across Molly's face. "Nay, no savages here!" She clutched her baby and turned away, looking at me over her shoulder.

"I promise. When we meet with Indians, it will be in Easton, not here. Thank thee, Peter, Molly," I said. "I won't abuse thy friendship."

I hid the wagon in their barn, unhitched and watered the horse, and led him to pasture. They invited me to stay for supper, but it would be a long walk back to Easton, and I still had to find a place to camp.

Back in Easton, hostility hung in the air. I saw local people taunting drunken Indians outside taverns. Did the Indians understand enough English to know they were being insulted?

Ahead, I heard shouts and screams. A fight! I pushed my way through the crowd.

Two men with knives were circling each other, one a

villager, the other a Delaware. The white man called out insults with the crowd's encouragement. The Delaware's eyes glittered with hatred, his jaw clenched.

From the back, a man yelled, "Kill him! The only good redskin is a dead redskin!" The crowd shouted their approval.

Villagers added their own taunts. "Go for him, John! Filthy thief! Murderer!"

John McCowen was one of the brawlers, and the other was Broken Blade! I knew they would kill each other if they could.

Without thinking, I flung myself between them and shoved them apart. "*NO!*" I shouted. "*STOP IT!*"

The two froze, each with a knife poised to stab. Two knives ready now to come down on me! I had a hand on each panting chest. My arm span was all that was keeping them from murdering each other. How long could I hold them apart? I couldn't back out. Neither could I think what in the world to do next.

John didn't even recognize me. He was set to kill whoever kept him from killing a redskin. Just as his knife plunged toward my neck, Broken Blade shoved me out of the way. As I sprawled to the ground, a man barged through the crowd and called out something in an Indian tongue.

I looked up.

"Christopher!" I cried. "Thank God!"

I've never felt so relieved to see anyone. Even his physical presence was enough to break up the fight. Best of all, he could speak the Lenapé language, and he knew Broken Blade.

Broken Blade had saved my life, just as Christopher

had said he would. But he was still ready to kill John. Christopher held him back.

Then John realized who I was and what he had nearly done to me. "Noble! Good God, man! Ye nearly got yerself killed!" He pulled me to my feet and threw his arms around me. It was good he held me up, because my knees were like rubber.

Christopher took charge. He led the three of us out of the street into a cleared space. Realizing the fight was over, the crowd dwindled away.

Christopher spoke sternly to Broken Blade, who sank to the ground cross-legged, still scowling. Then Christopher turned to John and me and repeated in English what he had just said. "What started this fight?"

"This savage killed my friend Robert! He's wearing Robert's hat." John lunged for Broken Blade again, but I held him back.

Christopher turned to the Delaware and translated John's accusation.

Broken Blade's jaw dropped in disbelief. Then he protested, and Christopher translated for us. "He says he's had this hat for years, and it's true. I've seen him wear it."

"That's Robert's hat!" John insisted. "Everybody knows these heathens lie and steal. If Robert was here, he'd snatch it from him. Are you taking his word against mine?"

Without understanding a thing John said, Broken Blade knew he had not been believed. He glared defiantly at John. Then suddenly he seemed to recognize him. He started talking fast to Christopher and pointing to John. Even without understanding a word of it, I knew from his gestures that he was telling about attacking John on the mountainside. Then he pointed to me and must have been telling about my rescuing him when the beech branch pinned him to the cliff.

A wry smile came over Christopher's face. "Noble," he said, "it seems that each of these men owes you his life, and each would like to kill the other. What do you have to say?"

"I didn't save them so they could kill each other, or anyone else, for that matter."

John burst out, "This heathen skunk killed Robert! I know he did."

Christopher repeated what John had said, and then Broken Blade let loose a torrent of frustration.

Christopher shook his head sadly and turned back to John and me.

"What did he say?" demanded John.

"He said he might have killed your friend. He has killed lots of settlers, he says."

John made a lunge in the Indian's direction. Broken Blade sprang to his feet with a snarl. Christopher and I restrained them, and then Christopher continued.

"He's being honest, at least, so listen to him. Their leader, Teedyuskung, talked them into these raids, but now he wants peace. That means no more of your friends would be killed. Both sides have grievances that will have to be settled. But street fights could ruin the peace conference."

"Please, John," I pleaded. "We've been working toward this conference for months. Give it a chance."

Broken Blade wanted to know what we were saying, so Christopher translated. Broken Blade argued with him. Christopher rolled his eyes and shook his head in frustration. Turning to us, Christopher said, "I'm going back to his camp with him. See you around. It's going to be an interesting week!"

"Ye should never try to break up a knife fight by yerself, Noble," John said as we walked toward the center of Easton. "I know you Quakers don't believe in fighting, but ye could have got yerself killed. It's somewhat a miracle that both of us didn't stab ye when ye run between us like that."

"It felt like a miracle to me! If Christopher hadn't come along just then, I might not be walking with thee now."

"Who is Christopher, anyway? How do ye know him?"

"He was the scout for the wagon train trip to Wills's Creek. You met him then, but you were so out of your head those days that you don't remember him. He knows the tribes well and works now as a translator."

"What did he mean when he said each of us owed you our lives? I know ye saved me when that savage left me fer dead, but how does *he* owe ye?"

I really didn't want to tell that story. I remembered Jedediah's scorn when he heard it, and John would probably be even worse. I kicked a small rock ahead of me as we walked, stalling for time. But John would not be put off.

"C'mon, Noble. What happened?"

"Does thee remember when Enoch and I first found thee on the road? Thee was out of thy head with fever, so thee may not. Thee wouldn't go with us unless we brought thy pelts."

"Aye, I remember that much."

"Just as I finished emptying the cave, a beech branch crashed down right near the opening. There was an Indian behind the branch staring right at me. I thought he'd kill me, he looked so fierce, but then I realized he was pinned. The branch had landed on his foot."

"He woulda kilt ye, fer sure, if he could. Was it this same one?"

"Aye. I remember the wolf tattoo on his face."

"So how does he owe ye his life? Ye didn't release him, surely?"

I nodded, concentrating on kicking the stone down the street.

"Noble! Ye didn't!"

"He was wounded, John! I couldn't leave him there. He would have died! Thee was wounded, too, and we didn't leave thee."

"Unbelievable! You Quakers are astonishin'! Did ye not think of the lives he would take? And he has taken 'em. I'm sure he was in the party that attacked me friend Robert. Ye saved a bloodthirsty savage, and Robert, who never hurt no one, is dead because of yer tender heart! And no tellin' how many others yer heathen has kilt!"

I sighed. I didn't expect John to understand, but still I tried to justify myself. "He was suffering. I did what I felt led to do."

John shook his head in disbelief. "And now yer workin' fer Pemberton tryin' to make peace. Well, I wish ye success. There's been overmuch of killin'. Peace would be welcome."

"Then help us, John."

"Huh! What d'ye think *I* could do? I'm in the militia, guardin' the governor and protectin' the neighbors."

For a few seconds I just stood silent in the middle of the street. Then I took a deep breath, turned, and looked John straight in the eye.

"Try to believe that peace is possible," I said, and then I stopped. I didn't want to say too much.

"So if we all believe peace is possible, it will happen?" John's voice oozed sarcasm.

"Well, it's not likely to happen if no one believes there's a chance for it. Doesn't thee think that, all things being equal, most people want to live peaceably?"

"But what's 'equal' between us and redskins? What do they understand about peace? They're savages, less than human!"

"They are not savages! They lived in peace with us for seventy years. Something has upset them and turned them violent. When we find the cause and address it, we can have peace again."

"Ye mean we should just give 'em whatever they want and then they'll leave us be?"

"What does *thee* want John? What keeps thee in such a rage all the time?"

He paused and gazed off into the sultry haze. Then his anger spilled out.

"Three times now me family has been run off, once by British, once by Quakers, and now by stinkin' heathen. I want land for me family and for meself. I want no one to challenge me right to it. I'll pay for it, fair and square—I'm not askin' anything fer free—but I want to feel secure in ownin' it. I want to marry yer sister and raise a family without fear of bein' attacked or run off our land. Is that askin' too much?"

"Sounds reasonable enough to me. I'm pretty sure

it's the same answer any Indian would give to the same question. Friend Pemberton says that if everyone is given a fair deal they will respect each other's rights and live peacefully together."

"Trouble is, we want the same land," John admitted.

"Aye. So what could thee give up to get what thee wants, and what would thee absolutely not give in on? That's how negotiating works."

"If they'd leave me alone, leave *us* alone, I could leave them alone."

"Could thee, really, John? It would mean respecting their rights and not assuming they're up to no good. Could thee do that?"

"I don't know. They've already killed a bunch of people and done a heap of damage." His voice rose in resentment.

"We have done the same to them, so they don't know if they should let us alone, either. That's what this conference is about, trying to figure out what would make each side feel secure enough to leave the other alone. If we can figure that out, peace may have a chance."

"And you Quakers think you can do better than the governor can?"

I nodded. "We have proof that the governor and the Proprietors have been taking advantage of the tribes. We're here to keep the government honest and convince the Indians of our good will."

"So that's what yer really up to. But ye still haven't answered me question."

I was surprised. "Ask it again."

"What can *I* be doin' fer peace?"

"No more street fights."

John grinned sheepishly and shook my hand. "It'll be hard, but I'll work on it."

We walked in silence a while, and then John said, "Where are ye stayin'?"

"I still have to find a place."

"C'mon, then. Ye can bunk wi' me at the ferry house. Ye're skinny enow to fit in the corner. Ye scarce could find a room elsewhere these days. B'sides, a lone Quaker lad could find himself attacked by some of the local bullies. They've no use for yer people. I'd better keep an eye on ye meself."

So John led me to the ferry house of Nathaniel Vernon, his employer. Besides being the office for the ferry, it was also an inn over a tavern, and this week it was full to overflowing.

"Does thee have room? It looks like not one more person could even squeeze into the taproom."

"Aye, the help (that's me) stays in the cellar, and I doubt Mr. Vernon would put anyone in with us. But the place is full, for sure. We've got government people, a few Quakers, even Indians stayin' here. Mr. Vernon's been put in charge of feedin' the Indians, so ye'll see plenty of them savages hangin' around."

"Delaware, John," I corrected him.

"Right," he said. "I'll try to remember. But it won't be easy. Wait till t'night when ye see 'em lollin' around outside waitin' for someone to hand 'em a drink. Then you may call 'em savages yerself. Not a pretty sight!"

I didn't answer, but I knew Broken Blade was *not* a savage. I owed my life to him now, as he had owed his to me. Would I get a chance to thank him?

CHAPTER 25

The Peace Conference

The peace conference began the next day. Every time Governor Morris moved from his lodging to the town square or back again, he had his own parade. First came the color bearer with the flag of England, followed by the fife and drum corps tweedling and thumping away, then the governor himself, surrounded by the brightly uniformed Royal American Regiment, and finally the rag-tag Provincial Troops. I saw John and Peter trying to keep step, each wearing what was probably his best shirt, decorated with a bit of red ribbon.

Suddenly Molly appeared at my elbow, Molly and baby Sarah.

"Good day, Noble," she said. "Peter said I should ask you to look after me and Sarah while he's on duty. I wouldn't stay by meself on the farm fer fear of yer Indians."

I laughed in spite of myself. "They're not *my* Indians, but I'll keep an eye on Peter's ladies. I'm on duty myself, though, so if Friend Pemberton needs me, I'll have to leave thee."

She nodded, satisfied.

From the opposite direction the Indians came, single file, led by King Teedyuskung.

"Look at their leader wearin' that fancy greatcoat!" Molly exclaimed. "And trimmed in gold lace! Who do you suppose he killed to get that?"

A woman standing next to her said, "Someone said the French had given him the coat and that he wore it to threaten the governor."

"Oh, aye, as if to say 'Make peace with us or we'll go over to the French.'"

"Fancy as it is," the other woman said, "it doesn't look like much over those cheap checkered pants and riding boots."

The two of them kept up a running commentary as Teedyuskung passed us. He walked stiffly, as though the boots hurt his feet. He must have been sweltering in the heat. I was, for sure.

The rest of the Indian delegates wore only breech-clouts. Their moccasins were decorated with porcupine quills, and their heads were shaved except for topknots decorated with single feathers. They stared straight ahead, and no one could read their faces. I saw Broken Blade, but he didn't look in my direction.

The Quakers came last, not at all in formation, quietly talking among themselves and shuffling papers.

There was no building in Easton big enough for this conference, so men had built an open shelter under a huge tree in the middle of town. The governor and his advisors sat at a plank table facing the Indians. The Quakers were behind the Indians. About a hundred other Indians were standing in the shade, men, women, and children, alert, ready for anything. The rest of the square and beyond was filled with locals. They didn't want to miss all the excitement.

I stood to the side where I could see Friend Pemberton if he signaled me for an errand.

The formal speeches began, complete with wampum. The crowd was fairly quiet, though I could hear oooh's and aaah's when Teedyuskung gave the governor strings of wampum to open his eyes and clear his throat. The governor thanked him with a flowery speech of his own, but then he said that Conrad Weiser, the number one interpreter, hadn't arrived yet, and he didn't want to do any business until Weiser came.

Teedyuskung agreed to wait. Then Governor Morris invited the Indian king of ten nations, as he called himself, to dine with him. That was the end of the first session, and the parade wound its way back. Peter came back to claim his little family, and I found Friend Pemberton.

"Isn't this a day wasted?" I asked. "Thee came to make peace, and now thee must wait until tomorrow."

Pemberton smiled. "Patience, Noble. We'll improve the time by 'polishing the chain of friendship,' as the Indians say. I won't need thee today. Enjoy thy day off."

Every day followed the same pattern, a big parade, a short public meeting, and adjournment, followed by the return parade. And every day Molly came with little Sarah and stood beside me until Peter was ready to go back to the farm. Sarah slept through most of it, and when Molly got tired of holding her, she gave her to me. So there I stood, next to a woman and holding her child. I felt kind of squirmy about it. Would people think Sarah belonged to me?

Molly was unconcerned. She followed the course of the conference, and when she didn't understand what was going on, she asked questions I couldn't answer. During the return parade, she talked about whatever came into her head. One day it was all about her garden. Another time it was about her childhood back in Ireland. Then on Thursday, she started telling me about her man Charley.

"Charley and Peter got to be friends," she said. "When Peter caught up with General Braddock's army, one of the first people he met was Charley. He told 'im I was back at Fort Cumberland, and Charley was glad to hear it. Peter doesn't talk about the battle. He just told me that when Charley died, the last word out of his mouth was 'Molly.' And when the army finally straggled back to Fort Cumberland, it was Peter that told me Charley was dead."

"I'm sorry," I said.

She brushed tears from her eyes. "I didn't know what to do with meself. I couldna go back to Philadelphia because I had run away. I woulda been thrown in gaol fer sure. But Peter said I could go home with him and work for his family. Then on the way back, we decided to wed. And now here I am, a married woman with a wee one to raise. Who ever would'a thought a year ago that I'd be here now?"

"Or me, either," I said. "I never would have dreamed what has happened since we left thee at Fort Cumberland." Then I stopped myself. I didn't need to tell Molly or anyone else my story.

Friend Pemberton didn't need me all week, because all the people he wanted to talk with were right there in his inn. He did pay my regular wages, though.

Most people who weren't official delegates spent their evenings at taverns drinking and carousing. They thought it was great fun to get Indians drunk and then take advantage of them. Teedyuskung was the only one who could hold his liquor. We heard he could drink a gallon of rum a day and still not be drunk. Quakers pleaded with the Indians to stay sober, but it didn't do much good.

When John was off duty, he and I walked around Easton because it was too crowded and noisy in the taverns and too hot to go to sleep. He introduced me to his mother, who was cooking for Bachmann, and his father, working for Vernon. They both thanked me for saving John's life and wished my family well. Nice people. His mother was so careworn and frazzled that I wished Ma could give her a cup of tea. His father looked like a fierce eagle, seemed to be angry all the time, but there was a twinkle in his eyes that I would have loved to see in Pa's.

John and I talked some about our dreams for the future. Sheba was on his mind a lot, I noticed. I never asked him about repaying my loan, and he never mentioned it. I did tell him I was still saving money for tools and described the few I had. I told him I hoped to work for William Savery in a few months. He just nodded and then asked again about Sheba.

We ran into Christopher during one of our evening walks. I asked him about Broken Blade.

"He's been keeping to himself a lot this week. When I advised him to stay away from the taverns, he had already decided not to go in. He won't touch liquor, he says. He's seen what it does to people, and he wants none of that."

"I'd really like to thank him for saving my life the other day."

"That's decent of ye, Noble, and it may work out, but don't count on it. Just because he saved yer life doesn't mean he's yer friend. He was just doin' what he had to do as a good Delaware."

"I wish we spoke the same language."

"Wantin' to put me out of work, are ye?" Christopher said. "Well, I wish we all spoke the same language. It might make gettin' along a heap easier."

"What goes on at these dinners after the peace talks adjourn?" I asked. I hoped I wasn't out of line to question him, but I cared so much and knew so little.

"The food is good, but not as good as in Philadelphia," he joked.

Seeing I was disappointed at being put off, he leaned his back and one foot against the side of a building and began to explain. John was as interested as I was.

"Usually it's private talks so Quakers can explain to Indians what really went on during the day. Then the Indians change what they've agreed to or lay out what they'll say the next day."

John had been hanging around while we talked, trying not to be embarrassed by the fight Christopher and I had broken up. Now he said, "I heard the governor banned the Quakers from visiting the Indians."

"Aye, he did, but he couldn't ban the Indians from visiting the Quakers. Quakers feed them well. Indians can always put away a meal."

"What are the chances for peace?" I asked.

"Too soon to tell."

On Friday, a courier from Philadelphia brought big news. After two years of threats, England had finally declared war on France. When the governor learned of it, he read the proclamation after the opening of the afternoon peace talks. He made it sound like very good news, and the American Regimentals fired their guns in celebration. That scared the Indians! They ran for cover, women and children screaming. But then things calmed down again.

Except for little Sarah. Molly was holding her when the guns went off, and the baby couldn't stop crying. Molly bounced her on her shoulder, but she wouldn't stop. Her squalling grew loud enough for everyone in the square to hear. Molly worked her way to the edge of the crowd. I followed, feeling responsible to look after the two of them. Finally she stopped under some trees near the Indian women and children. Turning her back to me, she began to nurse the baby.

I could hear Sarah sucking greedily, insistently, as if wolfing down a workingman's meal. Suddenly she jerked her head back, and I saw her little face twist. Her arms and legs thrashed so wildly that Molly nearly dropped her. Then Sarah stopped breathing. Her whole body went limp. Her lips started turning blue.

"Sarah!" Molly screamed, terrified. She shook the baby, trying to revive her. Wildly, she looked around for help.

What happened next seemed as slow as molasses oozing over a block of ice compared to the thoughts popcorning in my head. An Indian woman ran from out of nowhere and snatched Sarah! Was she kidnapping her under our very eyes? My worst nightmare was unfolding right here in the peace conference! And I couldn't move fast enough to stop that heathen from murdering an innocent baby! Not just any innocent baby! Sarah, who a few minutes ago was safe in my own arms.

The savage flipped Sarah over and turned her face down. Was there a knife in her hand? Would she stab her or cut her head off? Again I saw severed baby heads still in their little caps out in the back country. I could hear Molly still screaming Sarah's name. I tried to push my way through the crowd of Indians.

Holding one hand under the baby's belly, that vicious redskin slapped Sarah's little back with her other hand as fast as she could. Why was she torturing her like that? The least she could do was wait till she was out of sight. If Molly saw that heathen kill her baby, she would never get over it. And I knew I wouldn't, either. It felt like iron weights were dragging my arms and legs as I tried to move forward. I saw Broken Blade watching intently, but he didn't move.

The heathen squaw paused a second, but Sarah was limp in her hands. Dead, I knew. Poor Sarah! Poor Molly and Peter! And who would be attacked next? All this going on just a few feet from the peace table! I could hear the fife and drums of the departing parade. No one in authority knew what was happening.

Again that terrible savage pounded away between the baby's shoulders. Sarah was dead. Why keep hitting her? What kind of people could do such a thing to a little baby? I kept pressing forward.

At last I broke through the group, just in time to see Sarah shudder, take a deep breath, and begin to cry.

The Indian woman smiled, handed Sarah back to Molly, and vanished into the crowd.

Peter had heard Molly scream, and he pushed his way toward her. By the time he got there, Molly was hugging Sarah and craning her neck to find the woman who had saved her life.

"What happened?" Peter asked.

"She brought her back!" Molly exclaimed. "But I can't find her to thank her."

"Someone tried to steal our baby?"

"No! She stopped breathing, and I didn't know what to do. An Indian . . ." Words failed her, and she pantomimed with her hands how the woman had rescued Sarah from certain death. "I want to thank her, but she's disappeared."

This Indian woman, not a savage, not a heathen, not a terrible, cruel person, had saved Sarah's life! As that certainty sank in, I was ashamed of how I had assumed the worst, ashamed of the awful names I had called her in my mind. If I, who wanted peace so much, had jumped to the wrong conclusion, what did that say about the chances for peace among people who weren't so sure they wanted peace at all?

CHAPTER 26

Peace?

It turned out that the Friday session adjourned the peace conference.

"Isn't that ironic?" Israel Pemberton said. "Ending a peace conference with a declaration of war!"

All that hard work: Philadelphians coming to Easton, Indians walking all those miles, the turmoil in Easton, the expense of gifts, the cost of lodging and meals, the countless errands I had run. After all that, had we produced no solid results?

"Has thee failed, then?" I asked him.

"Nay, I wouldn't say 'failed.' We've made some progress. Now that England has declared war on France, the government needs the Indians badly enough to be generous with supplies. The governor insisted that the Delaware return all their white prisoners, and he has promised many gifts when they do. They are desperately poor and need all the gifts we can offer. Both sides have agreed to meet here again in October. We Friends will do what we can to keep the government honest."

"Is it time now to give them the gifts we brought?"

"Aye. Have the wagon here in the morning. We'll leave for home when it's unloaded."

So I spent the night with Peter and Molly. Sarah was fine, as if she hadn't nearly choked to death. Peter helped me hitch up the wagon to go back to Easton, and Molly packed a lunch for me to eat on the road home.

"Goodbye, Peter, Molly," I said. "Thanks for thy hospitality. Take good care of little Sarah. Mayhap we'll meet again some day."

Peter shook my hand, and Molly planted a kiss on my cheek. "It's been good seein' ye again, Noble," she said.

I didn't feel anything. Nothing! I knew I'd not be bothered by dreams of Molly again. I nodded and climbed onto the buckboard.

I delivered the wagonload of gifts to Friend Pemberton, who handed them over to the governor to distribute to the Indians. He gave Governor Morris an itemized list of all that the Quakers had donated and wanted him to pass it on to the Delaware, but the governor refused. Instead, he announced that many of the gifts had come from Friends.

The Indians were happy with what we brought, but Teedyuskung took it a step further. He said to the governor, "We will deliver these gifts to our brothers and sisters in the mountains and not keep them all to ourselves. We are too few to carry all this, though. We need a horse to carry some of them."

So Governor Morris had to find a horse for Teedyuskung. But it was not a packhorse. Teedyuskung himself rode it out of town, and somehow the Indians managed to carry all our gifts.

Friend Pemberton went back inside Bachmann's inn. As I waited at the foot of the steps, I saw John coming up the road, a large leather bag on his shoulder. His face beamed as he slung it onto the ground in front of me with a metallic clank.

"I bet ye thought I'd forgot I owed ye for bailin' me out of gaol, Noble. Well, of course I hadn't, but I have an offer for ye. I'm tryin' to save whatever cash I can to buy some land. Then I can marry Sheba and offer her a home. You, on the other hand, want money for tools, as I recall. So I wonder, would ye accept my poor friend Robert's woodworking tools in lieu of cash? I claimed 'em for ye, if they'll do ye any good."

With that, he grabbed the bag by its bottom corners and dumped the contents out in a jumble. "Will these help ye, Noble?"

I dropped to my knees amid the tools and quickly set them in order. There were three sets of clamps, chisels of all sorts, four kinds of saws, a miter box, a t-square, a plumb bob, two braces and a variety of bits, several different planes, and a glue pot. Robert must have been a master cabinetmaker to have owned these fine tools.

"Oh, John! These are worth far more than I loaned thee! I can't afford them."

"Nay, ye don't understand. These are yers if ye can use them. They cost me naught. Robert had no heirs, and there's no reason ye shouldn't have 'em if ye want 'em. Think of it as payment for every good thing ye ever did fer me, such as savin' me life not once but twice, takin' me home to mend, introducin' me to yer sister, the love of me life, *and* bailin' me out of gaol. I want ye to have 'em, and I'll still be in yer debt fer as long as ever I live."

Here, spread out on the ground in front of me, were all the tools I would ever need. Here was my future in the present! I didn't know what to say.

Then John added, with a grin, "And as yer Pa would

say, 'No sense goin' home with an empty wagon.' After unloadin' all them gifts for the Indians, Israel Pemberton will surely have space for a bag of tools."

I laughed and laughed. It was either that or cry. Then, stalling until I could trust my voice, I gathered the tools carefully back into the bag. At last I managed to say, "Yes! Yes, of course I can use them! Thank thee, John! Thank thee so much. Keep thy money, and as soon as thee can marry Sheba, I'll be the first to welcome thee as brother!"

Then John added, "And would ye have room for me in the wagon as well? There's naught fer me here in Easton. 'Tis a quarrelsome place, and I've had me fill of it. My stint with the militia is up, and I thought to hitch a ride w' ye as far as the city and then make me way to yer Pa's farm. I'd like to work fer him and finish me apprenticeship as a cordwainer. Mayhap I'll even learn the peaceable ways of Quakers while I'm at it."

I threw my arms around my friend and pounded him on the back. Friend Pemberton quickly agreed to John's riding back with me, and John left to get his things. We would meet at the ferry.

Christopher came to say goodbye.

"Thank thee for thy good work this week, Christopher," Pemberton said. "Thee is one of the best translators we've had."

"How's that, sir?" Christopher asked.

"Because not only does thee know the Indian tongues, thee knows both their ways and our purpose. I appreciated thy interpretation as much as thy translation this week."

"Thank you, sir," Christopher replied. "I did the best I could for both sides. You want peace, but the Delaware *need* peace. They're near to starvation because of all the troubles. I doubt the gifts you brought will get them through the winter."

"If Teedyuskung keeps his promise to return English prisoners, they will get all they need. We Friends will see to that," Pemberton assured him.

"Will he keep his word, Christopher?" I asked.

"I have to wonder about that myself. I hadn't even heard of Teedyuskung before this year and never laid eyes on him until this conference. He seems to have come from out of nowhere, making grand statements about being king of ten tribes. I have to wonder."

Friend Pemberton said, "Our government has given him a large unfinished belt of wampum to take to the tribes east of the Susquehanna, inviting all of them to come to another conference here in three months. On their side, they understand that they must return all English prisoners they hold."

"Aye," interjected Christopher. "They understand that. But I didn't hear them promise. From what I've seen, those prisoners may be so taken with Indian ways by now that they might refuse to return."

"What if they don't return the English prisoners?" I asked.

Friend Pemberton and Christopher exchanged tired smiles. "Then there will be another conference, and another, and another," Pemberton said. "We will never give up."

"Noble, what you yourself did may be the best thing that happened all week," Christopher said.

"What does thee mean? I've only run errands."

"When you stopped that fight, you did more than keep those two from killing each other. If that had happened, the peace conference would have fallen apart before it began. In camp that night, another Delaware who saw the fight told the rest about it. The way he told it, your stopping the fight proved that your people were serious about wanting peace."

"What is thee talking about, Christopher?" Israel Pemberton asked. "Has Noble been a hero and I haven't heard of it?"

I shook my head and scuffled my shoes in the dust. "I hate to think what might have happened if thee hadn't showed up just then, Christopher."

Christopher told Friend Pemberton how I had tried to break up John and Broken Blade's fight that first evening.

"Noble, thee continues to amaze me," Pemberton said with a broad smile. "Christopher is right. Thee is a peacemaker thyself. If all of us had thy courage and compassion, there would be no need for peace conferences. Thee has lived thy name this week."

I was astonished. I had sometimes dreamed of hearing that, but I never expected it would happen. "It's only my grandmother's family name, not a description," I stammered.

"Thee is too modest," Pemberton said. "What could be more noble than risking one's life to save another, let alone two, let alone the entire peace process?"

"But I didn't think about risking my life," I said. "I just jumped in and pushed them apart. Then when I realized where I was, I was scared to death! If Christopher hadn't come along at the right time, John would have killed me."

"Of course thee was frightened. I should think so, indeed!" Pemberton said. "But that takes nothing away from thy noble actions. In fact, it fairly defines nobility: doing what is right without considering the risk to oneself. Would thee agree, Christopher?"

Christopher looked at me with a smile. "Aye, I would define 'noble' just that way meself. You did it, even if ye didn't consider it ahead of time. I'm glad I was there when ye needed me."

That was way too much praise for me to handle. To sort of change the subject, I asked again, "So has thee achieved any degree of peace?"

"It's a beginning, Noble," Pemberton said. "It's an uncertain peace. It all depends on everyone's keeping his word. That's where we stand at this moment."

At that moment, I knew where I stood. I stood for peace, and I'd work for it always, even as a cabinetmaker. No more fence sitting for me. I had a new sense of my own worth, too, at least what these two good men thought of me. I could live with that.

AUTHOR'S NOTE

The events of this book are taken from issues of Benjamin Franklin's *Pennsylvania Gazette* and *The Colonial Records of Pennsylvania.* The Walking Purchase occurred in 1737. In 1755 there was a wagon train to supply General Braddock, and the political positions of the Quakers and the Proprietary Parties of the Pennsylvania Assembly are factual. Bodies were dumped on the steps of the Assembly Hall to motivate Assembly members to defend the colony. Pennsylvania did declare war on the Delaware tribe and offer bounties for scalps. Israel Pemberton did mount a Quaker effort to achieve peace, and the peace conference at Easton occurred as described.

The Butler family and John McCowen, Susannah and James Wright, Colonel Innis, the McDowells, John Harris, the Pemberton family, Jonathan Mifflin, William Savery, Conrad Weiser, Scarouady and the other Indians at Pembertons' house, Teedyuskung, and of course Benjamin Franklin are all real people of that time period. Broken Blade, Jedediah, Christopher, Molly, Peter, and the Pembertons' servants are fictional, though their actions are appropriate to the story and to the times. John did marry Sheba, in 1759. Noble married Susannah Beale in 1763. In 1777, during the war for American independence, John, Sheba, Noble, and Susannah moved with their children to Wrightsboro, Georgia, another story for another time.

DISCUSSION QUESTIONS AND SUGGESTED RESEARCH TOPICS

PROLOGUE (p. vii)

What have you learned about Noble and Pa? How are their interests and values different from each other's?

Suggested Research Topics: Colonial apprenticeships, Quaker use of "thee" and "thy" (They didn't use "thou.")

CHAPTER 1 Wagoners Wanted (p. 1)

How does Noble present his big idea to the family? What do you think are Pa's strongest values? Is Will right that making money on war is as bad as fighting? What are Noble's values about war, family, and money? What happens when teens question family values?

Suggested Research Topics: *The Pennsylvania Gazette*, colonial mills, Quaker pacifism, colonial kitchens, rope-strung bed, French and Indian War

CHAPTER 2 The First Day (p. 9)

How do you think Noble and Enoch will get along on the trip to Wills's Creek? What does Pa mean when he says, "Don't come home with an empty wagon"? In what ways is the city overwhelming to Noble? Is Enoch affected in the same way? What is Noble's impression of Benjamin Franklin? At the end of the chapter, Noble wonders why Pa let him go on this trip. Why do you think Pa did?

Suggested Research Topics: Conestoga wagons, clothing in colonial times, colonial taverns, trenchers, Fort Cumberland (Maryland)

CHAPTER 3 The Edge of the West (p. 19)

How does dinner in Lancaster differ from dinner at the Three Ships Tavern in Philadelphia? Why does Susannah Wright feel safe on the frontier? What dangers does she see? What peoples face such dangers today?

Suggested Research Topics: Lancaster County, Susquehanna River, Susannah Wright

CHAPTER 4 Crossing the Susquehanna (p. 24)

Why was Molly a member of the wagon train? Why was Noble uncomfortable talking with her? Why did Peter join the wagon train? What is Daniel's attitude toward Quakers? Why was getting acquainted with the other wagoners unusual for Noble? As Noble goes beyond his family's values, what is he risking? What, if anything, is he gaining? For the first time, Noble encounters prejudice against Quakers. How do you evaluate his reaction? How does Enoch respond? What causes prejudice? What other kinds of prejudice do you notice in this story?

Suggested Research Topics: Indentured servants, Colonial Assembly of Pennsylvania

CHAPTER 5 Storm (p. 34)

Why did the wagoners kill the pigeons? Why did Noble react as he did? The storm itself is a kind of violence. How does Noble respond to this situation? What do you think will be his reaction to future violence?

Suggested Research Topics: Passenger pigeons, what happens when lightning strikes a tree

CHAPTER 6 **Stories in the Rain** (p. 39)

What does Horst's story tell you about how and why there were so many German immigrants in colonial Pennsylvania? How did William Penn's sons' behavior differ from their father's? Why does Christopher's attitude toward Indians differ from Daniel's? Is Daniel right that a government must protect its people? Other than militarily, how else can a government do that?

Suggested Research Topics: European feudal system, trans-Atlantic crossings in the eighteenth century, William Penn and the Delaware Indians

CHAPTER 7 **Peter's Wagon** (p. 48)

Where does Noble stand now? What does he think he's worth? Do you agree? What might have happened to Peter if he had returned on his own? Why do you think it was Horst who offered him a seat? How did Peter think his father would react to the loss of his wagon and horses? Do you think Horst and Jedediah convinced him otherwise? How does Noble feel about Molly? Why? What kind of relationship do you think they will have?

Suggested Research Topics: Tow ropes, early roads

CHAPTER 8 **Massacre** (p. 55)

The horror of the massacre raises many questions for Noble. Discuss how something this violent makes him feel inadequate. How would you answer the questions Noble asks himself in this chapter? In what ways are his reactions similar to those we feel today when a violent crime is committed?

Suggested Research Topics: Potomac River, Indian attacks on Pennsylvania settlers in the eighteenth century

CHAPTER 9 Fort Cumberland (p. 60)

How did Fort Cumberland differ from Noble's expectations? What difference did it make (to the wagon train, to the people at the fort, to Molly) that General Braddock had already left? Why, in your opinion, did Peter join the militia? What did Noble want from his conversation with Enoch? How would you answer the questions Noble raised?

Suggested Research Topics: Colonial fort architecture, Allegheny Mountains

CHAPTER 10 Rescues in the Forest (p. 69)

How was the wagon train different on the return trip? Do you think the Pennsylvania colonial government agents acted appropriately at Burnt Cabins? Explain your answer. Would you have stopped to help John McCowen? Why did John resist help? Noble had to make some quick decisions in this chapter. How did he make them? Would you have made the same choices he did? Was he honest with Enoch and Christopher?

Suggested Research Topics: Burnt Cabins (PA), leather tanning in colonial times

CHAPTER 11 McDowell's Mill (p. 81)

Describe the first aid treatment Mrs. McDowell gave John. Do you expect him to survive? How do you think John felt when he learned his family had fled? Do you think Mrs. McDowell was cruel in refusing to keep John? What would you and your family do in a like situation? How do Jedediah and Christopher respond when Noble tells them he freed the Indian? What is Broken Blade's obligation now? How do you think it will play out? Christopher says Broken Blade has reason to be bitter (towards whites). What reason might he have? Noble falls asleep thinking about responsibility and hospitality. What do those terms mean to you?

Suggested Research Topics: Colonial medical treatments, Indian scouts, Wyoming Valley (PA)

CHAPTER 12 The Way Home (p. 90)

Why did John hesitate to go home with Noble and Enoch? How are John's story and Broken Blade's story similar? Explain what Noble means when he says, "Even people who hadn't taken other people's property get sucked into fighting." How do you define "manhood"? Why is Noble uncomfortable talking about Molly? How has the trip to Wills's Creek changed the way Noble thinks? How many of his new insights do you agree with? How has his relationship with Enoch changed? Why?

Suggested Research Topics: Scotch-Irish settlers in Pennsylvania, the Clearances in Scotland, John Harris

CHAPTER 13 Home at Last (p. 102)

Compare Ma's medical care with that of Mrs. McDowell. How did Noble feel about being back home again? What is Holy Conversation? Does anyone practice this today? How did Pa know where Enoch and Noble should sell John's pelts? When Benjamin wants details about the trip, Noble thinks, "The most important part was what I'd thought about, what I'd learned." Is he the same person he was when he left? What is Noble's definition of being a man? Do you agree with it?

Suggested Research Topics: medicinal use of leeches, Quaker Holy Conversation, colonial monetary systems

CHAPTER 14 Settling Up (p. 108)

What is Pa's grand plan for his sons? Should parents plan their children's futures? Why or why not? Both Enoch and Noble seem to reject Pa's plan. Are their lives better or happier than if they had followed Pa's plan? Enoch tells Noble that they must give John the whole amount from the sale of pelts and let him give them their share. Why was that important? Is that what you would have done? Why does Mifflin give them prices in both pounds and Spanish dollars? Noble's tantrum seems uncharacteristic. Do you think it is justified? What does Franklin offer instead of pay? Why won't Noble ask Mifflin for credit? What do you suppose Noble wrote in his account book that night?

Suggested Research Topics: Colonial woodworking tools

CHAPTER 15 The Longest Summer (p. 117)

What is the significance of the title of this book? How do you think Noble feels about John and Sheba falling in love? What is the Butler family's reaction to news about General Braddock's defeat? Why does John react so differently from his hosts? Do you agree with him that "you Quakers have the blood of all these brave soldiers on yer hands"? Were they guilty? How would you respond to such an indictment?

Suggested Research Topics: eighteenth century shoemaking, farm tools, spinning wool, Fort DuQuesne, General Braddock

CHAPTER 16 A New Job (p. 126)

Do you think Noble is responsible for what Broken Blade might be doing? Christopher tells Noble, "You just have to live with the consequences of being true to your beliefs." Choose one of your beliefs and consider what might be the consequences of being true to it. How does Noble respond to Peter's news? What motivated Noble to ask Mifflin about a job as a woodworker? If woodworking is what he really wants to do, why did he ask Pemberton for a job as a runner? Do you think this was wise or not? Why? What does it mean to shake hands on a job offer?

Suggested Research Topics: Israel Pemberton Jr., the Library Company of Philadepphia, almshouses, the Fire Company of Philadelphia

CHAPTER 17 **Israel Pemberton** (p. 138)

Describe how Noble might have felt coming from the farm to the city, from a middle class farm family to a very wealthy one. What kind of things did he learn on the job? What is a birthright Quaker? How much courage do you think it took for Noble to ask Pemberton about the questions bothering him? Were Pemberton's answers satisfying to Noble? To you? Pemberton says, "Friends believe the best way to prevent violence is to deal fairly and kindly." Is this applicable to situations today? If so, which ones?

Suggested Research Topics: James Pemberton, Franklin's post office, Carpenters' Hall, Conrad Weiser, Defense Quakers, George Fox

CHAPTER 18 **Outside the Meeting** (p. 146)

Why was the man driving back and forth in front of the Quaker meeting house? Do you agree with his reasoning? Do you think Israel Pemberton's response was appropriate? What did Noble think of it? Once again, Noble has an argument with himself about freeing someone. What did he risk this time? Do you think he made the right choice? Were you surprised by Pemberton's response? What is going on in Easton, according to John? Why won't John stay at Pemberton's? Do you agree with his reasoning?

Suggested Research Topics: Quaker meeting houses, eighteenth century prisons in colonial America

CHAPTER 19 **What Friends Can Do** (p. 158)

How well do you think Pemberton lives up to his Quaker beliefs? Do you think Pemberton is responsible for violence on the frontier? Why or why not? How does Noble feel when he realizes Pemberton is tormented by the same questions that torment him? Describe the deadlock between the

Assembly and the governor. What was the resolution? Was it true to Quaker beliefs?

Suggested Research Topics: Governor Morris in 1755–56, Iroquois Indians and their relation to Delaware Indians

CHAPTER 20 The Light of God Within (p. 162)

What has happened to Noble's ambition to become a cabinetmaker? What do you think Pa will do if Noble doesn't come home for spring planting? How does Pemberton reassure Noble? Does Noble agree with his reasoning? Do you?

Suggested Research Topics: Quaker names for days and months

CHAPTER 21 The Past Revealed (p. 166)

What insight does Pemberton have about the cause of Indian attacks? In what ways is he working against his own government? Is it right for a private citizen to take such matters in his own hands? Can you think of any current examples of this kind of activity? In what ways does Noble think Pemberton and Pa are similar? What new insights does Noble have about his own activities of the past year? Pemberton seems to have become almost another father to Noble. Describe how an adult other than your parents has influenced you.

Suggested Research Topics: Bounties, land purchases in colonial Pennsylvania

CHAPTER 22 The Future Unfolds (p. 172)

How does Noble feel about Indians coming to Pembertons' house? What reservations does Christopher have about participating in the dinner? How could Pa's arrival disrupt the meeting? How does Noble react to noticing Pa's bald spot? Why is this important to him? Why does Noble keep his voice low? How effective do you think this is? What reasons does Pa offer for Noble's disobedience? When Pa asks for the balance in Noble's account book, Noble reflects on all the questions he has asked himself. What does he mean by "Back to the snake fence"? How does Pa respond to Noble's answer? What was your response? How did Pemberton's dinner end?

Suggested Research Topics: Andrew Montour, Scarouady, gazebo, wampum

CHAPTER 23 **Preparations for Peace** (p. 183)

Describe the relationships between the Delaware and the Iroquois and between the English settlers and the Iroquois and Delaware. Conrad Weiser warns Pemberton that he is in danger of working against his own government. Do you agree with Pemberton's response? Scarouady announces the Iroquois will send a delegation to the Delaware. What are the dangers of this trip? What are the dangers if they don't go? How might Noble's visit to William Savery's shop be a turning point?

Suggested Research Topics: Onondaga, chain of friendship, Sir William Johnson, William Savery, lathe

CHAPTER 24 **Easton** (p. 191)

How is this trip different from the trip to Wills's Creek? Why is Noble trying not to think of Molly? What are his feelings for her at this point? There is a saying that wealth has its privileges. How does Pemberton exemplify this? Again Noble runs into prejudice against Quakers. How does it affect his relationship with Peter and Molly? How has Molly changed? How does Noble justify the Quakers' presence at the peace conference? Was Noble brave or foolish to break up the fight? What does John claim is the reason for the fight? Do you believe him? What is Broken Blade's response? How does believing that peace is possible help the peace process? How does Noble's asking John what he wants turn the conversation? How, according to Noble, does negotiating work? How is this applicable to other peace conferences or private issues?

Suggested Research Topics: Easton, PA, in 1756, Durham Forge, smelting, pig iron, quicksilver

CHAPTER 25 The Peace Conference (p. 206)

Describe the daily course of the peace talks. Where was any progress being made? What kind of activities went on outside the talks? Christopher tells Noble that Broken Blade isn't necessarily his friend, even though he has saved his life. What are the implications of that statement for the peace process? Describe Noble's feelings as he watches the Indian woman with Sarah and afterward when he sees the results of her actions.

Suggested Research Topics: Teedyuskung, French and Indian War

CHAPTER 26 Peace? (p. 215)

At the session on Friday, guns are fired to salute the declaration of war against France. Discuss the irony of this ending to the peace conference. Discuss the resolution of Noble's feelings for Molly. Were you surprised? Did John's repayment of Noble's loan seem appropriate to you? Why are people doubtful about Teedyuskung? What is Pemberton's definition of "noble"? Do you agree with it? What do you think Noble wrote in his account book after this event?

Suggested Research Topics: Peace Conferences at Easton, PA, in October, 1756, and 1758

ACKNOWLEDGEMENTS

Much of the fun of writing this book has been doing the research. I wish to thank those who helped: the staff and volunteers of the Colonial Pennsylvania Plantation in Ridley Creek State Park in Media, PA, where I have set the Butler family farm in this story; the staff of the Friends Historical Library of Swarthmore College, who welcomed me day after day and provided invaluable assistance—especially Historian Chris Densmore, who read the manuscript for historical accuracy and taught me a great deal; the Special Collections Library of Haverford College, where I was allowed to transcribe the minutes of the dinners with the Iroquois at the home of Israel Pemberton; the Chester County Historical Society; the Historical Society of Pennsylvania; the Library Company of Philadelphia; the American Philosophical Society in Philadelphia; the National Historical Park of Philadelphia and their staff for special tours; the Northampton County Historical Society; the curator of the Susannah Wright House in Columbia, PA; and the staff in the Map Room of the British Library in London, who were amused by my enthusiasm.

The Highlights Foundation has helped my development as a writer, especially through their Historical Fiction for Young Adults workshop where I was mentored by Liza Ketchum and the late Ellen Levine. My writers groups in Pennsylvania and in Florida have guided me patiently through many versions of this story.

My deep gratitude goes to Chel Avery, my editor, who believed in my story and brought it to fruition.

Most of all, I want to thank my husband, Thomas Olshewsky, for his encouragement and unflagging interest in my project and for teaching me advanced research skills. Not many spouses would cheerfully agree to move to another city for an indeterminate time so I could pursue my dream. His experience as a professor and writer has lighted my path and kept me going.

ABOUT THE AUTHOR

Janet Olshewsky, an Indiana native, has taught English and social studies to high school students in Indiana, Illinois, Ohio, and Florida. She and her husband, Thomas Olshewsky, live in Sarasota, Florida. They have seven children and four grandchildren between them.

To research this book, Janet and Thom moved to Pennsylvania for nine years. Janet volunteered for the education program of the Colonial Pennsylvania Plantation where she learned open hearth cooking, spinning, and candle making. She traveled the route of Noble's journeys to Fort Cumblerland and Easton. Her research took her to the Historical Society of Pennsylvania, the Friends Historical Library of Swarthmore College, the Chester County (PA) Historical Society, the Northampton (PA) Historical and Genealogical Society, and the British Library in London.

Janet is available for school visits in authentic colonial costume. She can speak with students about the issues raised in *The Snake Fence*, about the colonial period, and about conducting historical research and the writing process. Visit her website at www.janetolshewsky.com.

She is also the author of *More than an Average Guy: The Story of Larry Patton.*

CPSIA information can be obtained at www.ICGtesting.com
Printed in the USA
LVOW081214070413

327981LV00002B/219/P